There
Was
Still
Love

Also by Favel Parrett

Past the Shallows
When the Night Comes

Favel Parrett

There Was Still Love

SCEPTRE

Originally published in 2019 by Hachette Australia
First published in Great Britain in 2020 by Sceptre
An Imprint of Hodder & Stoughton
An Hachette UK company

1

A CIP catalogue record for this title is available from the British Library

Hardback ISBN 9781529343557
eBook ISBN 9781529343564

Typeset in Garamond Pro

Printed and bound in Great Britain by Clays Ltd, Elcograf S.p.A.

Hodder & Stoughton policy is to use papers that are natural, renewable
and recyclable products and made from wood grown in sustainable forests.
The logging and manufacturing processes are expected to conform to the
environmental regulations of the country of origin.

Hodder & Stoughton Ltd
Carmelite House
50 Victoria Embankment
London EC4Y 0DZ

www.sceptrebooks.co.uk

For DK – my love

And for my grandparents, Mitzi and Bill –
who were the very best of people

The Suitcase

There are suitcases everywhere. They cover the country. Little brown suitcases on trains, and on carts – suitcases strapped to the top of buses. There are suitcases being carried along old country roads by women, by men, dragged by children. There are suitcases abandoned in ditches, suitcases left broken in stairwells.

People carry little brown suitcases.

Inside, all they can hold. A set of warm clothes, a photograph of loved ones, a treasured book. They carry little suitcases to imagined safety and hope to find a place where they can put their suitcase down and unpack.

You must become a little brown suitcase.

You must close up tight, protect your most needed possessions – all you can hold. Your heart, your mind, your soul. You must become a little suitcase and try not to think about home.

Melbourne

1980

Our footsteps echo as we climb the stairs. My grandma holds my hand.

Shhhhh – be quiet! My grandpa is sleeping.

The third floor flat, the heavy wooden door, and, inside, the smell of warm pipe tobacco and homemade cakes. Home.

Take your coat off – hang it on the coat rack. Take your shoes off – put them in the shoe rack. Put on your slippers. Mine are red and my grandma's are blue. My grandpa's are brown, but they are in his room where he is sleeping.

Down the hall, past my grandma's bedroom and past my grandpa's bedroom, past the green-tiled bathroom, and into the small, light kitchen. My grandma puts the cloth shopping bag on the table. It has flowers on it and zips up into a small leather wallet when it's not being used. It is a good bag and it holds a lot. It comes from Czechoslovakia.

I unpack the shopping. Three Kaiser rolls. A wrapped paper parcel with six slices of Swiss cheese inside. A paper parcel with six slices of Pariser sausage inside. A loaf of rye bread with caraway seeds. A jar of Nova gherkins. One round black and green tin – Dr Pat pipe tobacco for my grandpa.

My grandma fills up the kettle over the sink and sets it on the stove. She lights a match and the gas ring explodes blue – *pooof.* That sweet smell of gas. My grandma blows out the match, then breaks it in half with her fingers. She drops the broken match into a glass ashtray. It's full of match halves – one half clean; the other blackened and burnt.

I hear the toilet flush. My grandpa is awake.

My grandma scoops loose tea into the shiny teapot. She smiles at me and then begins to sing.

> 'One-two-three
> Grandma caught a flea
> Put it in the teapot
> Made a cup of tea
> The flea jumped out
> Grandma gave a shout
> Here comes grandpa with his shirt hanging out!'

I join in with the last line, and just like that – my grandpa opens the kitchen door. He's wearing his white singlet and striped pyjama bottoms and his brown slippers – his face still puffy with sleep. I laugh at his crazy sticking-up hair, at the way he always looks so surprised to be alive. He sits down at the green table next to me. He pats my head.

My grandma makes the tea.

I'm sailing across space – far from Earth – and there is nothing but black and the distant light from stars that shine. But I can see her now, just in view – the little bright-blue planet. Neptune.

A flute plays. The keys of the celesta chime.

I fly faster, I move with speed and the planet gets bigger, brighter, until there is nothing else but blue.

High voices begin to sing, a dream calling me – pulling me in. I reach out my arms, my fingers. Closer, closer – I try so hard to touch the surface, but the celesta chimes again, and Neptune begins to fade. She becomes see-through, translucent, and my hand slips right through.

The singing becomes softer, quieter – softer, until there is no longer any difference between sound and silence.

Dappled light through the lace curtains. The ticking of the Smiths clock.

I'm sitting on the upside-down cream footstool – my spaceship. Three wooden legs stick up in a triangle around me, little metal feet on the end of each like antennae.

The tape in the stereo runs fast to its end and clicks off. Everything is still. The coffee table, the TV with the lace doily on top, the sofa underneath the double windows, the gas heater, the mantelpiece, the framed tapestry of a city far away – with bridges and a river and a castle and a dark sky. The third storey flat.

My whole world.

My grandpa's heavy breaths. He is asleep in his armchair. I stand up and look at him. So peaceful, his face smoothed down with sleep, his arms crossed on his lap. I don't want to wake him, but he opens his eyes.

'Malá Liška,' he says.

That's me. *Little Fox.*

My grandpa sits up and taps his pipe out in the ashtray – the contents grey and long gone out.

'Did the tape finish?' he asks, and I nod.

Side two – the best side. Saturn, the Bringer of Old Age; Uranus, The Magician; Neptune, The Mystic – my favourite planet, and *our* favourite piece. My grandpa thinks that the celesta is a magical instrument and I always listen out for it in each different track. Holst: *The Planets.*

My grandma calls out from the kitchen. Lunch is ready, and my grandpa stands up, stretches his back. He takes my hand. We walk together to the kitchen for our lunch – a Kaiser roll with a slice of cheese and a slice of Pariser, a whole dill gherkin on the side. One gherkin for me, one for my grandma and one for my grandpa.

———⚡———

Silver coins in a jar. An old Nova gherkin jar.

Nova gherkins were the best ones. After The Curtain came down, we couldn't seem to get them anymore. I never found a gherkin that was as good as those Czechoslovakian Nova gherkins – not even close. I used to eat one every day with my lunch and I would always save it until last, until I had finished my roll, because then the taste of the gherkin lasted longer. Sometimes when my grandma was asleep in her chair, my grandpa would sneak one out of the jar and crunch it down quickly with the fridge door open. He really loved those gherkins.

But every gherkin was rationed. And every fifty-cent piece counted.

My grandpa would sort through his coins in the late afternoon before he had to get ready for his night shift at the factory where he was a night watchman. He'd take his dinner with him – two tin plates together like a clamshell. My grandma's cooking, rich with butter and salt and fried, golden goodness.

My grandparents saved their fifty-cent coins to buy aeroplane tickets. They managed to do this every four years, sometimes every three years if they were very careful. If they saved hard.

They bought the cheapest tickets.

They took the longest route.

In that small, dark travel agent on Elizabeth Street, near the old market stinking with meat and cheese and fish, a Greek man held out the book of tickets for my grandpa to study. My grandma held my hand.

'Melbourne – Sing-a-pore-*re*.

'Sing-a-pore-*re* – Athens.

'Athens – Frank-a-*furt*.

'Frank-a-*furt* – Praa-*g*.'

Forty-two hours.

My grandpa hated flying. He got claustrophobic and paced and sweated and tried to calm himself by smoking his pipe. Then smoking was banned. Things were worse for him after smoking was banned. He had to fight the urge to smash the window or open the emergency door and jump out. It was a battle to hold on. Sometimes he thought he might start screaming. But he never did. He made it – every time. He wanted so badly to go home.

Luděk

MAY 1980

Pigeons – there are five hundred million pigeons in this city. They shit on everything. They shit on the sculptures, on the heads of all those stone saints. The famous people from history are covered in shit. Once a pigeon shat on Babi's head, but it never happens to him. He is too quick, he runs too fast and the shit never gets him.

He is invisible. It is his super power.

He can fly through the streets, move past eyes, unnoticed.

He can slip right under the heavy blanket that covers this city – the fear cannot touch him.

Luděk is free.

And he sees everything.

A teenage girl in a tight yellow skirt is blowing bubbles in the square – little rainbow spheres of light. Two girls with the same long hair are trying to clap the bubbles dead in their hands. They are screeching, laughing – smashing the bubbles between their red, sticky palms. But some of the bubbles get away, rise up high and fly above the city. They fly with the birds that look down. Maybe some even make it all the way across the river. Luděk does not know. He cannot see that far.

The tower clangs – once, twice – Luděk feels each strike of the clock right in his guts. It shakes him into action. Three times, four. *Clang!* It's 5 pm. The day is falling away right in front of him. He is not meant to be over this side – not so far away from home. And there is only one hour left before he has to be flying up those stairs to the flat. One golden hour.

He runs through the tower and onto the bridge. It is already busy with workers – men moving in their dark suits, women in skirts, spring coats, handbags, satchels, shoes, boots. Two old-timers are already drunk, tripping and slipping over their own feet. What jokers. *Go home and get out of my way!*

Luděk weaves his way through the crowd with stealth. He knows the statues on the bridge by heart. He has names for them all and he yells at each one as he runs.

'Hey Fat Guts! Hey Stupid! Hi Dumb-Dumb! Hey Sleepy! Hey Hunchback! Hey Squint Eyes!'

The only statue he likes is the lady with the pointy crown, and he never yells insults at her. He calls her by

her name, Bar-ba-ra. Barbara, my Barbara! He likes the
way that name makes his mouth move.

Bar – ba – rah!

A woman stops in front of him and looks around.
He must have yelled that last Barbara a bit too loudly. He
moves faster. Babi would kill him if she found out he
was yelling at saints. He would get the wooden spoon for
sure AND no dinner. She would tell him that the statues
would get their revenge on him. But he does not believe
any of those old stories, the ones about the statues coming
to life in the night. He is not a baby. The statues are just
old, dead stone. They are not going anywhere in a hurry.

'Up yours, Pointy!' he yells at St Augustine, then he cuts
a hard left and zips down the zig-zag stairs two steps at a
time. He's on the home side now, and there is time for his
favourite place – the Kampa.

A lady in a fur coat is taking up the whole path. Luděk
darts around her and nearly trips over a little dog – *Sorry
little dog!* He smiles at it.

Dogs. There are lots of dogs out now. Fancy dogs,
fluffy dogs, big bruiser dogs. Luděk loves them all. God,
he wants a dog. He would be happy with any kind of
dog. It *does not* matter to him. Whatever dog came along,
he would love it. Even if it was the ugliest, dumbest dog
in the world, it would still be better than no dog. He has
never seen a dog he did not like. And they like him, too.
They see him even when people do not. He is not invisible
to dogs. Dogs take notice.

Sometimes he wants a dog so badly he thinks about just stealing one – one that's mistreated and left out in the cold. He knows he can't have one, not while he lives with Babi, and he never even asks about it. But maybe if Mama came back they could get a dog. If she came back and did not go away anymore maybe it could happen. A friend, one that could run as fast as he could.

The path is stuffed with prams, and babies are screaming their heads off. One thing Luděk *does not* want is a brother or a sister. He does not want a bloody baby. NO WAY! He'd be stuck with it; like the other kids in the park, stuck pushing a pram around. *Look after your brother. Look after your sister. The baby needs fresh air!*

He gets away from the prams, away from the screaming babies, and he keeps moving. He is almost at the best bit of the park now, where all the lovers are, where all the smoochers meet.

At his favourite tree, he catches his breath. He scans the scene.

The after-work love-fest.

Couples slouching on park benches, leaning against trees in the shadows. Hugging, kissing like they are hungry. All those hands moving under tight dresses, under tight shirts, hands squeezing flesh. So many lovers everywhere like it is the national sport.

He cannot stop watching.

'Lov . . . vers.'

A loud voice behind him.

Luděk swings around. An old man – his eyes sloppy and drunk, his face crazy.

'Lov . . . vers,' the man says again with his open, dribbling mouth.

Luděk takes off, he runs flat out. He hears the man yell out again, but he does not look back. He runs until he can hardly breathe. When he is far enough away, when he is safe, he slows down. There is an empty glass bottle of Kofola on the ground and Luděk kicks it hard. It clatters along the pavement and flips up onto the grass without breaking.

Why did that old madman have to wreck everything? Why did he have to be there? Drunken idiot.

He takes the path towards the exit closest to the flat and he keeps his eyes peeled for squirrels. The trees are full of leaves and the park is looking good. The end of spring. Summer holidays are just around the corner.

A couple walk towards him on the path in the beginning shadows. They are holding hands. They stand out in the open – together. They are not groping in corners or hiding behind bushes. They are not afraid.

They move past him silently, like they are floating, and they are not looking ahead, or at the trees, and they are not looking at Luděk. They just stare into each other's eyes, and their eyes are soft and they are smiling.

Luděk can feel it. They are in love.

The street lights flick on, the ones that aren't busted, and despite himself, his hand makes a fist and he pumps it into the air.

There is still love. And there is still cake, sometimes.

The world can do what it likes. The world can go to hell for all he cares because Babi is waiting for him in the warm flat. His whole world.

Luděk holds onto this feeling with everything he has. He packs it tightly down inside himself. Then he turns and runs down the lane towards home as fast as his legs can carry him.

Prague
1980

Mama's car – the pea-green Wartburg. Uncle Bohdan had it now. God, he was a terrible driver, always going seventy miles per hour no matter what. And Babi made things worse. *Turn here – watch the road – go that way – slow down!*

Uncle Bohdan would just keep driving fast and he would not say one word while Babi yelled on and on. He would just sit there and take it, his hands tight on the steering wheel, his eyes fixed ahead. Luděk felt a bit sorry for him then, even if it was true that he was useless at driving. Luděk had been thrown forward so many times because Uncle Bohdan was always slamming on the brakes.

When Mama was home, Luděk sat in the front seat next to her. He liked being able to look through the wide bubble windscreen, and when it rained she would let him turn on the windscreen wipers, and he would watch them move back and forth in rhythm, wiping the fat drops of water away.

Babi made him sit in the back, and he could sit on the left or on the right or even on the tiny middle seat if he wanted to. No one bothered him or paid him any notice when he was in the back. He could even lie down if he wanted to, across the whole back seat. But when Babi and Uncle Bohdan lit up their cigarettes, the back seat became a speeding smoke chamber. He would have to sit up then and keep his nose close to the seam of the window to get air. That was the only way he didn't turn green. Babi never let anyone open any of the windows in the car in case the breeze messed up her hair. Luděk didn't think any amount of wind could make her hair move because she used so much hairspray, but there was no point arguing with Babi. Anyway, the car sickness was worth it because they were going to the airport. Luděk loved going to the airport.

Big planes landing, big planes taking off. Planes flying to cities far, far away. Luděk liked to think about all the places they came from, and all the places they flew to. He had never been on a plane. He would probably never go on a plane, and he understood that. But going to the airport was still a big deal. It always felt like something important might happen, that someone famous might be there, or Mama might finally be coming home.

He watched the glass doors at the airport open and close, open and close.

People walked through dressed up in their best suits, in their best dresses and shoes, suitcases piled on trolleys. The families waiting for them were always crying, calling out, waving their arms in the air. It was like a serial on the TV, one that Babi would like, one that Babi would make him watch with her – the same scene played out over and over and over.

Luděk wasn't sure he could remember the last time Aunty Máňa and Uncle Bill came. He didn't know how long they had stayed or where they'd slept, or what had happened for the whole six weeks of summer holidays. But he did remember the presents. A red Matchbox car, two t-shirts with English words on them, and his fluffy sheepskin slippers.

He had grown out of those slippers in less than six months and that was a real blow because they were just so good. They still looked practically new – good and warm and soft, but they were useless now. His feet grew too fast. Babi said she could see them growing right in front of her eyes. Maybe Aunty Máňa and Uncle Bill had brought him something as good this time. Luděk hoped for another Matchbox car.

When they finally came through the sliding doors, it seemed like they were walking in slow motion. They looked lost, their eyes vacant. Babi started to cry, and called out – and then Aunty Máňa put her hands on her cheeks and started crying, too. They both stood there hugging and crying right in the way of everyone. That was a bit embarrassing – two old ladies standing there crying.

Uncle Bohdan stepped forward and took control of the trolley. Three suitcases. Maybe there really would be a lot of presents.

Uncle Bill walked towards Luděk.

'Nice to meet you,' he said, and he put out his hand. Luděk shook it.

'And your name is?'

Luděk grinned. 'Luděk,' he said. 'It's me, Luděk!'

Uncle Bill smiled. 'My God. What happened to the small boy I used to know? You are nearly as tall as me.'

Luděk kept on grinning. He was tall for his age but he would never catch Uncle Bill. Uncle Bill was some kind of giant.

Aunty Máňa's arms were around him now and she lifted him up off the ground. 'Luděk! Luděk! Luděk!' she said, and she kept saying his name like she was trying to make sure she would never forget it.

He looked at her face. She had the same face as Babi. Their mouths were the same, their lips downturned like an upside-down smile. And their eyes were the same, large and brown with flecks of green deep inside. They both had big faces, strong angular faces that you could grab onto with both hands. You could hang off those faces. Stone faces that could forge through anything. Faces you would never forget.

They were not delicate, but they were useful. They could withstand a lot.

Four adults, one child and three suitcases – Mama's pea-green Wartburg was at maximum capacity. Luděk was squashed in between Babi and Uncle Bill and it was a tight squeeze. To makes things worse, one of the suitcases was across his lap because only two could fit in the boot. Babi had made Aunty Máňa sit in the front so she could see everything properly.

'Look,' Babi kept saying, pointing out the window, 'The city – so dirty. See? Can you see?'

And Aunty Máňa kept making a 'Mmmmm' sound, and nodding her beehived head.

Luděk couldn't really see out of the window, but he hoped they were getting close to home. Now that all four of them were smoking in the car, the smoke chamber was worse than ever, and Uncle Bill smoked a pipe. But Uncle Bill put the window down a few inches and winked at Luděk. And Babi did not say one word about it.

Babi slept in the dining room on the single metal fold-out bed. Luděk told her she could have his room, and he would sleep on the fold-out bed, but she would not have it. She did not seem to mind anything when her sister was here. When her sister was here she was a different person. When her sister was here she was just happy. Anyway – the dining room was a nice room, one of the biggest rooms in the flat. It was where every single Christmas Eve feast had been. They never really used the room anymore – unless people stayed.

Luděk lay awake that night thinking about the presents.

There had been no Matchbox car, but there was a pair of jeans. Dark denim jeans, and a t-shirt with a yellow cartoon man on it holding a sword. There was also a winter jacket. The jacket was nothing like Luděk's old coat. It was like nothing he had ever seen. It was shiny and puffy and it had a thick metal zip and a hood to cover his head. It was like a spacesuit – grey with a navy blue stripe. Uncle Bill told him it was called a parka, and it was rainproof.

Everything was too big for him, the jeans and the t-shirt, and Babi made him put them away in the bottom drawer until he had grown a bit. That would not be long. By the time it was cold and the summer had gone, everything would fit. And the jacket didn't feel too big, just a bit long on the arms, and who cared about that anyway. Jackets were not meant to be tight. All the kids in the street would ask him where he got the jacket from and he would tell them that his great-uncle was a spy in THE WEST and that he brought Luděk clothes and toys and anything he needed all the way from Australia.

Luděk had seen a small girl in the photos Aunty Máňa brought with her, and he'd stared at the pictures, stared at the face. In one, the girl was wearing the same jacket he'd been given – only she was smaller than him, younger. She probably couldn't run around the streets by herself yet. Everybody called her Malá Liška, maybe because of her red hair.

Above the ticking clock, Luděk could hear Babi snoring in the dining room. He got up to go to the toilet and, out in the hall, he could hear that Aunty and Uncle were snoring their heads off, too. God, everyone was snoring. The whole flat was snoring. They had stayed up late talking and drinking and smoking and now they were all honking.

It was like sleeping in a pig barn.

Uncle Bill hardly spoke as they walked and that was fine. There had been too much talking in the flat. Babi and Aunty Máňa talked nonstop – *He did this. She did that. They got sick. Life is hard.* On and on – the endless drama. Old ladies. It was a relief to get away from them.

Uncle Bill was so tall, and he had long strides. The narrow streets seemed even narrower with him in them.

'Uncle?' Luděk asked. 'Where are we going?'

'Just call me Bill,' he said.

Luděk knew he had been called Bill for so long that he could no longer be anything else. But it would be hard to not call him Uncle. He would have to practise.

'I lost my name many years ago,' he said, and he looked ahead – the river in view. 'I lost my name, so I had to get a new one.'

Luděk did not know what his name had been before and he did not ask. They walked on together in silence down the long street.

'When you were a baby, I used to push you around in the stroller. Or sometimes I would just carry you,' Uncle Bill said. 'We would stay out for hours walking around this city. For the whole of summer.'

Luděk did not remember that, and it made him feel strange, the thought of being carried around and not knowing it. The thought of life going on before his memory existed.

'You never cried,' Uncle Bill said. 'You liked to be outside.'

They walked across the river, and into the Old Town. Uncle Bill led the way and he smoked his pipe and they did not talk.

Old streets that looked the same – cracks in the thin pavement; cracks in the apartment walls. A left turn. A right turn. A long one-way street.

A building faded yellow, stained grey. Wide windows and double wooden doors. Number seven. They stood there for a long time. Uncle Bill reached out and put his hand against the old wood of the doors.

'My place,' he said.

Luděk looked up at the building, at the three rows of windows. Three floors. There had been a boy and he had slept up there under the eaves of a large old flat. Only the boy had not been called Bill. He had been someone else back then.

Now there was an old man standing here.

He knew this place but it was not his place anymore.

Luděk sat across from Aunty Máňa at the kitchen table. He looked at her big, still face. It hung off her cheekbones – unmovable. Babi's face.

Aunty Máňa picked up her roll and took a bite. She chewed, swallowed, took a sip of her coffee – coffee she had brought in from the outside world. Instant coffee in a jar. It smelt sweet.

'Eat,' she said, just a small movement of her lips, and he took a roll from the basket, a boiled egg from the plate. Aunty Máňa pushed over the butter, the jar of apricot jam. Luděk buttered his roll, spread the jam on thick.

Uncle Bill was still in bed. He liked sleeping. He liked snoring. How did Aunty Máňa get any sleep? Luděk looked at her eyes and he suddenly wanted to ask her why she had left. Why she did not live here anymore.

He bit into his roll. He did not ask. He knew not to ask about THE WAR, about *before*. He did not say a word. He cracked his egg gently on the table, one – two – three. He started to peel it and the shell came away easily.

No one ever talked about *before*. Not even in whispers. Photos of *before* were hidden away in the back of cupboards. Stories from *before* were never told. *Before* had been forgotten, blacked out. But sometimes it was there if you looked carefully enough. There were little traces of *before* – like those gold and garnet earrings on Aunty Máňa's earlobes, the same as Babi's. Like that old suitcase in the roof space, battered and worn and locked up tight.

Luděk took a big bite of his egg. It needed salt, but there was no salt on the table. He did not want to move to get the salt from the cupboard. He did not want to break the connection that was there in that silence with Aunty Máňa.

She blinked. Her eyes stayed on his. They went in somewhere deep. He took a gulp of water and got the egg down. It was overcooked, the yolk chalky. Maybe he could just ask Uncle Bill about *before* – about what happened. He might get somewhere with Uncle Bill.

'It's good you are living here,' Aunty Máňa said. 'Your babi likes having you here.'

Luděk nodded. Yes, he liked it here. Yes, it was fine.

He took another sip of water and Aunty Máňa's eyes blinked again.

'But maybe you miss having a brother, a sister?' she said.

Luděk shook his head. No way. He *did not* want a baby – a brother or a sister. He was fine. Him and Babi. Just them.

He shook his head again. 'It's fine,' he said.

Aunty Máňa leant back in her chair. She drank the rest of her coffee. Her eyes were still on him, but she was far away now. She was far away and thinking.

Uncle Bill clumped into the kitchen, his face all pushed up on one side with sleep. He came over to the table and sat down. He reached out and slid Luděk's plate towards himself – the one with the half-eaten roll with butter and jam.

'Thank you,' he said.

Uncle Bill's daily joke. Luděk jumped up and grabbed his roll off the plate. He stuffed as much of it as he could in his mouth at once.

'Luděk!' Aunty Máňa said, 'you will choke!' But he kept chewing and his eyes laughed at Uncle Bill. *Get your own breakfast, old man!*

'Sit down! Chew properly!' Aunty Máňa ordered. And she whacked Uncle Bill on the shoulder. 'Idiot,' she said.

She got up from the table. Her hair was down; her hair was long and it ran all the way down her back. Aunty Máňa always wore it up, careful and neat, but sometimes in the early morning it was still loose and free. And the same bright-white streak of hair that Babi had went all the way from her scalp to the base of her back.

Aunty Máňa yawned, covered her mouth with her hand.

'Make your own *čaj*,' she said. Then she shuffled off in her slippers down the hall towards the bathroom.

Luděk lifted his cup off the table. He held it up in the air and waved it around in front of Uncle Bill's face.

'*Čaj! Čaj! Čaj!*' He chanted. 'Make me some *čaj!*'

Uncle Bill grabbed the cup out of Luděk's hands. 'You cheeky sod,' he said. And he said it just like that, in English, with an English accent. And it was so funny – that sound. So funny – those words, *cheeky sod*.

Luděk repeated the words out loud, laughing now, because they came out wrong in his mouth – 'Chee-kee so*d*. Chee-kee so*d*. Chee-kee so*d*.'

Another lazy summer day, and later he would walk with Uncle Bill along the streets and along the river and they would not talk. They would go to the park and Uncle Bill would sit and smoke his pipe while he watched Luděk climb trees and roll down hills and chuck himself off the biggest thing he could find. Luděk never grew tired of throwing himself off things. And later, Babi would look at the bruises on his knees, the cuts and grazes on his shins and palms, and she would shake her head. *How was it even possible?* Luděk did not know. He could not explain it, because in the rush and joy, in the moment of running and jumping and climbing trees, nothing hurt him. Nothing could touch him. Not one thing. There was nothing but energy – breath – movement. One more jump, one more flip, one more somersault in the air, then BANG – the ground, hard, cold and alive.

Luděk felt light-headed with the smell of schnitzels frying golden in the pan. God, Aunty Máňa was a good cook. He tried to hide his delight when she cooked for them because it upset Babi. It was the one subject that caused trouble between them. Luděk left it alone. He never asked what was for dinner or who was going to cook. BUT GOD he loved it when Aunty Máňa cooked. Even her vegetables tasted good. Even the carrots. Even the cabbage.

Babi said that Aunty Máňa was only good because she had worked as a maid in London and she had been taught.

'No one ever taught me how to cook,' she said. 'We had nothing. There wasn't even anything *to* cook.'

Aunty Máňa never responded when Babi said these things. She just watched her sister, her face serious, her mouth held still.

Luděk sat down at the table and Uncle Bill poured him a small glass of beer. Babi gave them both a look, but Luděk picked it up and took a sip anyway. It was like something sour and rotten washing around his mouth. He screwed up his eyes and put the glass down. Everyone laughed. Babi gave him a glass of water and he drank it.

Aunty Máňa put a schnitzel on his plate, some fried potato, and a big scoop of cucumber and cream salad. Luděk watched the cream flood the plate. That was the best thing – the taste of the cream salad mixed with the potato, the cream melting into the crispy schnitzel crumbs. It was all of his favourite foods on one plate and he could barely contain himself. The very second Uncle Bill began to eat, he inhaled his first mouthful.

Uncle Bill had a system. He ate everything evenly so that each different food on his plate disappeared at the same rate. This included whatever he was drinking. There was never more of one thing than another, and his last mouthful always included a bit of everything. Luděk had tried to copy this system a few times, but it was no good. What if you got full and you wasted your belly space eating cabbage? You might have to leave a dumpling behind, and someone else might eat it before you found room again. It was better to eat your favourite food first. All of it. Then your second favourite, and then the rest. Luděk ate his schnitzel first, all of it. The adults got two and he got one and there were no more left.

Luděk had no idea how Babi had gotten so much meat. She was trying her best to get everything for her sister, and the two of them stood in lines and shopped all day, chatting on and on all the while, and Luděk could not stand it if he had to go with them because everything took forever – every shop the same, every line the same – and even if he got a soft drink out of it or an ice-block, it was not worth it. They had run out of toilet paper, and it had been a three-day mission trekking around the streets to try and find some. They had to use cut-up newspaper and Uncle Bill said it hurt his *arse*. He told Luděk it was like going back to 'the bloody days of rationing'. Luděk had no idea what that meant. Babi was embarrassed, but there was nothing for it. There was no toilet paper in the whole Goddamn city, and no amount of money or haggling or wheeling and dealing could get you any. No matter how badly you needed it. No matter how much your arse hurt. That's the way it was.

Uncle Bill slipped Luděk his last bit of schnitzel, and Luděk scoffed it down.

God, Aunty Máňa was a good cook.

Luděk woke and it was dark. It was still night. He turned on his back and blinked his eyes until he found the ceiling, the walls, the outline of the room. He could hear voices in the lounge, soft voices.

He got out of bed and walked silently down the hall.

'You won't be able to come again. You might never be able to come back,' a voice said. It was Babi. Serious.

Then nothing.

Luděk breathed out. It was hot in the hall. His hands felt sweaty and he wiped them on his pyjama bottoms.

'What will happen to you?' A slight accent – a small hesitation. Aunty Máňa.

'I don't know.' Babi again and the sound of a cigarette being lit, a sharp exhale. 'She just has to get out.' Another pause, another exhale. 'She can't stand it anymore.'

Luděk felt something behind him, someone, and he turned quickly. Uncle Bill was towering over him.

34

'What are you doing up?' Uncle Bill said loudly, and the glass door slid open. Babi's hard face stared at him.

'Luděk! What are you doing?'

'I can't sleep,' he said, but it was no use.

'Bed!' Babi yelled. 'Right this second.'

Luděk knew he would not be able to sleep.

There was more talking, but it sounded like English. He tried hard to listen to the sounds, to the song. But he couldn't grasp it.

English. He did not know it. He did not like it. It was a dumb, flat song that he did not care to learn.

What were Babi and Aunty Máňa up so late talking about anyway? Why couldn't Aunty Máňa come back? No one ever told him anything. Like when Papa was sick and everyone just kept saying, *Papa is tired, Papa is resting.* And later, *Papa is sleeping.* Mama cried, and sometimes she screamed, and sometimes she just stayed in bed and couldn't see him even when he was standing right in front of her face.

He's just a small boy. He doesn't understand. He's just a small boy.

———

He stands in the hallway – just a small boy. Next to him is a little brown suitcase. Inside the suitcase are his pyjamas, his slippers, his toothbrush, his red toy car. His mama kisses him on the cheek. She is leaving him here.

'Can't I come with you?' he asks, but his mama is going far away with The Magician to places he cannot go. She has joined his theatre.

Babi takes his hand. They walk down the hall together, but the light above them goes out and his small hand slips from hers. Now he's falling, tumbling, down, down, and there's that suitcase again. But this suitcase is big. And this suitcase has fluorescent yellow eyes that stare at him.

'Your mama is inside,' a voice says. It's The Magician. It's his suitcase. And the suitcase opens up wide like a giant mouth.

There is nothing inside. It's just endless black, a void going on forever.

'Don't be afraid,' The Magician says.

He knows he must run. He must get away – but he topples and falls inside, and the black goes on forever.

'Mama!' he screams. 'Mama!' But she does not answer him. She is not there.

Uncle Bill lit a long match and held it to his pipe. He puffed hard until white smoke rose and the tobacco was burning.

He took the pipe out of his mouth, held it in his hand.

'I think that man is following us,' he said, and his eyes moved up the path towards another bench.

Luděk looked over at the man. He was wearing a dark overcoat and he had a briefcase by his feet. His black shoes were shiny.

Uncle Bill nudged Luděk gently, and Luděk looked away.

'I think I saw him at the airport,' Uncle Bill said.

Luděk remembered how Mama said *they* were always at the airport, watching, taking photos. She said there would probably be photos of him from all the times he had waited at the airport with Babi.

Uncle Bill blew out a big plume of smoke and it hovered in the air for a second before it moved off with the breeze.

'Well, he's free to watch us all he likes,' he said. 'He can take as many photos as he wants of us sitting here on this park bench. He can even take photos of me peeing for all I care.'

Luděk grinned and he kicked out his legs. He wanted to ask where the man hid the camera, and how he took photos without anyone seeing.

He looked up at Uncle Bill.

'Is it because of Mama?' he asked.

He meant because Mama was always overseas, and because she said that the system was rotten. And he thought about how Babi talked on the phone when Mama called. How she would say strange things that made no sense, like they were talking in another language, talking in code.

Babi told him to never say anything important on the telephone.

Uncle Bill smoked his pipe for a bit, and his eyes were unfocused like he was thinking of somewhere far away.

'Your mama has done nothing,' he said after a while. 'She is part of the famous Black Theatre and we should all be proud of that.'

Luděk nodded. Yes, it was good that Mama was showing the world how great their theatre was. His chest burned.

Uncle Bill continued to smoke. He took off his hat. Luděk looked at all the pigeon shit on the concrete path.

'Maybe it's because of me,' Uncle Bill said. 'This strange man comes here for six weeks and sits in the park and smokes his pipe. He does not work and he is not a tourist. He speaks Czech, and sometimes he has a small boy as an accomplice who can run very fast and jump from great heights.'

Luděk nodded. Yes, he could run fast. No one would ever catch him. He saw the man get up from his bench. He straightened his overcoat, checked the watch on his wrist, then walked slowly away down the path, briefcase in hand.

Luděk kept his eyes on the man until he was lost from view.

'Ah, maybe he's not following us,' Uncle Bill said. 'Maybe it was a different man I saw at the airport.' He tapped his pipe out against the bench railing and hot ash fell on the ground.

'But I have been watched before,' he said, and he looked down at Luděk. 'Because I was in the engineer's union.'

Luděk didn't know what Uncle Bill was talking about now.

'Nazis,' Uncle Bill said, and he handed Luděk a peppermint – one of the super-strong peppermints from Australia that he always kept in his pocket. They blew Luděk's head off every time, but he took one anyway. He could never resist.

'My father got me a job in London. Then my family were stuck here with the war, and they died with it, and that's how I thanked them.'

Uncle Bill looked away. He rubbed at his forehead.

They sat together sucking on their burning-hot peppermints as a group of workers in stained overalls shuffled past them after another long day of trying to fix rundown machines that belched black smoke and needed parts that would never arrive.

Luděk sat next to Uncle Bill on the crowded bus to Strahov. Uncle Bill was wearing his dark grey hat and his suit and he was reading the newspaper. Luděk had his comic out, but he was too busy to bother with it. He was too busy looking at all the people on the bus. Everyone was dressed up and alive and people were chatting and smiling and some people were even laughing. There was this electric buzz charging through the city like it was Christmas Eve.

Babi and Aunty Máňa had been up and ready since 6 am and they had both been yelling at Uncle Bill – telling him to get up, to get ready, to HURRY UP. Uncle Bill had wanted to stay home but he had no chance against the two of them. Luděk saw the back of their heads, up near the front of the bus, bobbing around with nonstop chit-chat. They were like little kids, all dressed up and going to the circus for the first time.

'I hate buses,' Uncle Bill said, and he folded his newspaper in half, put it on his lap. Luděk looked down at the screaming headlines.

Československá Spartakiáda 1980
Eight hundred thousand of our finest citizens will perform synchronised gymnastic routines at The Great Strahov Stadium – the largest stadium in the world! And the world will be watching.

'Is it really the largest stadium in the world?' Luděk asked.

Uncle Bill looked down at the newspaper and then at Luděk. He blinked. 'Eight football fields,' he said, 'that's how big it is.'

Eight football fields. Luděk couldn't even imagine that. He had never been before, to the stadium or to Spartakiáda. His school had trained for over a year to get in but they were not good enough. Some kids in his class had cried when they missed out, but the head gym teacher told them that only the best in the country could perform, so they must be happy and cheer their comrades on. Luděk guessed that kids in the country had nothing better to do than practise the synchronised dancing all day, every day, and he was glad when he didn't have to do it anymore. But today, with all the excitement, he thought that maybe it would be something to be out there performing in the big stadium.

'We will show the world how great our nation is,' the gym teacher had said.

The bus was in a long line of buses, and it kept stopping and starting and it seemed to take hours to get to the stadium. There were so many buses that it felt like maybe every bus in the whole country was right there – packed to bursting with bright faces.

Finally, it was their turn to pull up in the designated area, and Uncle Bill looked relieved to be outside. He lit his pipe. He took off his hat and slicked back his white hair, then he put his hat back on. There were people everywhere, it was like a festival or a giant summer market. Stalls and food and gangs of teenagers in uniforms, laughing and screaming and doing handstands on the concrete. Today, the city was full of young people. They had come from all over the country and they were all here to shine – nervous and excited and tanned and strong.

Babi held his arm tightly as they squeezed into line after line, and marched along bare concrete corridors booming with sound. It all looked the same, the stairs, the corridors, the walls – grey and plain. Each giant rectangular doorway they passed let in light from inside the open stadium, but none of them were their doorway. They walked for miles. Aunty Máňa's feet hurt. Babi was panting, but Uncle Bill just looked a bit pale. He took his hat off again and his hair was wet with sweat. There were so many people – all the bodies, all the legs, all the arms, all the sandals, all the white tennis shoes.

Section 8, row 12.

They had seats, lines marked out on the bare concrete benches: 20–24. They were near the top. There were standing sections below, but there was no way Babi and Aunty could stand all day. They sat down next to each other and Luděk knew they would not move again until it was all over and time to go home. He already needed to go to the loo.

Babi and Aunty took up more room than their two marked spaces on the bench, so Luděk was squashed into about half the space he should have had between Babi and Uncle Bill. Uncle Bill had strangers next to him and Luděk was glad he did not have to be squeezed in next to a strange man. Aunty Máňa had the end of the bench and that was the best seat. Luděk wanted that seat but he knew there was no chance. Anyway, he'd probably just get pushed off the bench completely from the combined weight and excitement of Babi and Aunty Máňa.

When they were finally seated, Luděk could take in the stadium. It was so large that he could not see all of it at once. It made him dizzy – the scale of it. The amount of people packed into it. A gigantic concrete rectangle as big as a city. It would probably take hours to walk around the outside. It would take forever. It was too much. It was too crazy. Luděk gripped the rough concrete seat with his fingers. What if you had to get out in a hurry? What if there was an evacuation? He looked down at his feet, at Uncle Bill's feet. Uncle Bill had shined his shoes.

There was a high-pitched squeal and the speakers crackled and popped and then a man's voice said, 'Welcome to Československá Spartakiáda 1980.'

The whole world erupted in clapping and the concrete ribs of the stadium shook. Everyone got to their feet as a giant flag of the nation was carried across the stadium floor and the national anthem rang out – *Where is my home, where is my home?* Babi was singing loudly with her hand pressed to her heart – *The Czech land, home of mine!* Aunty Máňa had her hand on her chest, too. But she wasn't singing. Uncle Bill's eyes were closed.

Fanfare, speeches, anticipation. Luděk waited for the spectacular to begin.

Parents and toddlers.

Parents and toddlers in overalls dancing together. Thousands of them moving side to side, some dumb song playing. Luděk's heart sank. Everyone was clapping after every few steps, after every circle formation. Was this what it was going to be like for the whole day? Luděk looked up at Uncle Bill. He was staring ahead, no expression. His eyes were not really watching as the toddlers and parents kept on dancing – side to side, round and round – all the same. All the same.

The kinder kids came on. More clapping. More 'Ooooohing'. More horrible music. Babi was swaying from side to side with the beat and pushing into him.

Uncle Bill's suit smelt like pipe tobacco and fried bacon. God, he really wanted something to eat. He really needed to go to the toilet. He tapped Babi on the shoulder but she shooed him off with her hand. Her eyes were large and full and she was following every single step. Aunty Máňa had her camera from Australia in her hands, and she was snapping away – in between rounds of clapping. Snap, snap. Applause. Luděk was pretty sure her photos would be terrible. They were so far away from the ground, the performers would look like ants. Ants wearing little green jumpsuits.

The sun was beating down. There was no cover – everything was open. It was lucky it was a clear day. Babi had told him that one Spartakiáda it had rained and the stadium floor was mud instead of packed dirt.

'Still the gymnasts went on,' she said, 'with muddy feet,' and she beamed with pride. With memories.

Luděk recognised the next song as it blasted out of the speakers. It was the song his class had trained to. Kids sprinted onto the field at full speed in blue uniforms carrying white hoops. Luděk knew the song by heart. He had had to dance to it twice a week for the whole year. It was such a stupid song – the stupid words, the stupid synth drums. And now here it was in concrete surround sound. He wondered if he knew any of the kids out there. He wondered how many boys called Luděk were dancing on the stadium floor. Maybe twenty. Maybe one hundred.

Another song – another thousand performers.

A moving ocean of colour.

'The women,' the commentator said, 'look at our women – their physical condition, their fitness, their athleticism.'

The crowd applauded.

Babi was beaming. Aunty Máňa took about five hundred more photos.

It was hard to believe they had both been out there prancing around in little, coloured leotards A LONG TIME AGO, when the stadium was made of wood and not concrete. But they had been.

'We used to perform. We used to be the best.' It was all they had talked about for days and they were still talking about it now. In between the clapping, in between the held breaths of anticipation. Oh, the nostalgia.

Sokol gymnastics. If you got Babi talking about Sokol, she would never shut up. Her eyes would light up and her hands would dance and she would go on and on. Somewhere hidden away in the roof was an old suitcase with a blue Sokol blazer inside, the emblem worn and faded but still there – *A Strong Mind in a Strong Body*. Aunty Máňa loved Sokol so much she had even planned to be a physical education teacher. Luděk imagined she would have been good at that. She would have enjoyed yelling orders at kids – *Higher! Straighter! Bend further. Keep in rhythm. Heads up! Eyes ahead.*

His mama could do all that stuff – move her body in crazy ways, bend her back right over. She could even put both legs over her head when she was sitting on the floor. Years of ballet, years of gymnastics. Years of pain and training.

'She could have been a great gymnast,' Babi always said, but his mama hated Spartakiáda, and she hated organised gymnastics. She just wanted to dance.

Uncle Bill stood up suddenly and he started to push past the knees of people sitting next to him. Babi stared up at him, covered her eyes from the sun with her hand.

'Take Luděk,' she said.

'I need to go to the toilet,' Luděk said.

'And get something to eat,' Babi yelled loudly, waving Luděk away, her eyes back on the stadium floor, on the giant creature made up of thousands of purple and white women.

Applause followed them down the concrete corridor. It was good to get away from the crowds, the sun. Uncle Bill lit his pipe, puffed heavily on it until it began to smoke white. He was sweating on his forehead. He looked down at Luděk's busting face and jiggling legs.

'Okay,' he said. 'Let's find the toilets.'

They sat in a canteen and Uncle Bill bought Luděk a sausage and an orange drink and he said, 'For Godsake, take your time eating so we don't have to go back out there.'

Luděk stabbed his sausage with the fork and took a bite. It was salty. Uncle Bill's sausage was covered in onions. Luděk hated onions. He only liked mustard but there was no mustard. He chewed slowly. The brassy music was coming through the speaker on the wall. On and on it went. On and on. Maybe there was still hours to go. Maybe they would be stuck here for days.

Luděk took a gulp of his drink. He knew Uncle Bill really hated the Spartakiáda. He hated all of it. But Luděk had seen him clap when the engineers came on. Just one clap but a clap all the same. The Engineers: Keeping the nation moving.

'Is the world really watching?' Luděk asked, suddenly remembering the newspaper.

Uncle Bill swallowed, wiped his mouth on a paper napkin.

'If Poland and Hungary and Russia are the world, then yes,' he said.

Luděk felt a bit disappointed then because he guessed it was pretty good even if it was a bit boring and long. The Union Collective had all these large metal curved ladders, and when they put them together, they made giant metal wheels. Men and women climbed on them and rolled around with the wheels, controlling them with strength and movement. And some of the formations had been good, the scale of them. All those giant pictures made out of people. Luděk didn't know how it was even possible to organise such a thing. How did they come up with it?

'We are invisible,' Uncle Bill said, and he looked down at his empty plate.

'No one knows we are here but us.'

At long last, it was the grand finale. Thousands of men in white shorts came running into the stadium screaming like warriors in battle. A mass of yelling topless men – The Nation's Soldiers: Bravery, difficulty, valiant battle.

Babi and Aunty Máňa went crazy. Babi was clapping so hard her cheeks were shaking. The soldiers must have sunbaked every single day to get that tanned. They were bronze like brand-new statues. They made pyramids of human strength, they held handstands for the longest time, they flew into the air like arrows, and tumbled and rolled. They were young and fit and strong and the applause grew like a fireball sweeping the stadium. Luděk's ears rang with it all the way home on the bus.

Spartakiáda was on TV about fifty times over the next week. Packages of it and highlights and even the whole damn thing. Uncle Bill refused to watch it. Luděk had to admit that it did look better on TV because at the stadium it had been impossible to see the details. At the stadium, you could only really appreciate the formations, the shapes. But on the TV you could see up close – the muscles, the strain, the incredible strength used. And you could see each human face. Not just one mass at all.

And at the end, the camera zoomed in on one soldier's face. He had blond hair, his skin beaded with sweat, and he closed his eyes and held himself still while the crowd roared and clapped and screamed. But then his mouth twitched, and for a brief moment, the young soldier smiled.

He had forgotten, in all the applause, that he was not a man. He was a soldier, part of the huge machine. And soldiers did not smile. He had forgotten that he was just a tiny part of the whole, and he was nothing without his comrades.

It was their last night already. Aunty Máňa and Uncle Bill were leaving in the morning before he'd be awake, and the summer had slipped away.

Luděk shook Uncle Bill's hand in the kitchen and said goodnight. It was a firm shake, a real one, Uncle Bill's large hand clasped tight around his. He would miss this man. This tall, booming man. It was like having his very own grandpa, one that did not boss him around or treat him like a baby. He had even played cards with Luděk and taught him a new game, one that he could play on his own when he was bored. It was called patience.

Uncle Bill let go of his hand.

'Don't ever take up smoking a pipe,' he said, and it was such a strange thing to say that it made Luděk laugh. Why the hell would he ever smoke a pipe?

Aunty Máňa grabbed him and hugged him so tightly that she nearly squeezed him to death. Then she asked if she could put him to bed because she wanted to tell him a story. He had not been told a story for a long time. He couldn't even remember how long. He guessed it had been one of Mama's stories.

He read to himself now that he was old enough, and Babi was proud that he could read. And he liked reading, but sometimes he missed stories being told to him – voice and words washing over him. He could close his eyes and rest and just listen. He would often fall asleep before the end of the story and never find out what happened. He would fall deep into the story somewhere along the way, and dream and fly until the morning.

Luděk lifted up the quilt and slid into his small bed. The sheets felt cool against his bare feet and he stretched his legs out.

Aunty Máňa sat on the bed. In the soft lamplight, she could have been Babi – her outline, her shape. She even smelt like Babi, like hairspray and talcum powder. It was only the slightest accent, the small hesitation in her words that gave her away every now and then. That pause told you that she had been away for a very long time, that she had been gone and only speaking her language in her dreams. And sometimes now the words did not come so easily to her mouth. Sometimes her words got lost and all she could do was stare after them and hope they would come back.

'Are you comfortable?' she asked, and Luděk nodded. He was impatient for the story to start.

'Well,' she said, 'on the darkest night, when there is a black moon, all the statues of Prague come to life.'

Luděk rolled his eyes. Not this old one again. Another story about statues coming to life and getting revenge. How dumb did Aunty think he was? He wished he could just read his own book now, and not be told baby stories.

Aunty Máňa cleared her voice. 'This is a story about a statue that came to life so he could save a small child from death.'

Luděk blinked against the lamplight.

'Do you know where the statue of Atlas is?' Aunty Máňa asked, and he shook his head. He had never seen this statue before. He did not know it.

'Atlas is not far away from where you sleep.'

'In the Kampa?' he asked. Maybe Atlas was a statue he had missed somehow.

'No, but close. He sits on top of an arched gateway, down a narrow lane, and he watches over a secret garden.'

'But where?' Luděk asked.

Aunty did not answer.

Maybe this *was* a new story, one Luděk did not know. Now he wanted to hear all of it. He wanted to know. He let himself sink down in his bed. He closed his eyes and listened.

'Did you know that Atlas is a Titan, a type of God, and he carries the whole of the sky and the heavens on his shoulders? He holds it all up using his incredible strength. And with great effort and strain, he keeps it above us. He does not let the celestial sphere fall down and crush the Earth.'

Luděk did not understand what a celestial sphere was, but he decided maybe it was just the sky – the sky and space and maybe the planets as well. Atlas, a God who held up space.

'A long time ago, there was a little girl who liked to play in the secret garden. One day she looked up and noticed Atlas for the first time. She saw the huge weight he carried on his shoulders and she felt so sorry for him. She could see the strain on his face, the strain in his large muscles, his bent over back. She decided she would come to the archway every day and talk to him. She would say hello and stand under Atlas so that he was not alone. Sometimes she would leave him a wildflower that she had picked. A white flower, sometimes a purple flower, sometimes a yellow one. She would leave the flowers at the bottom of the gate so Atlas could look down and see that she had been there.

'This girl visited Atlas for many months. And she wished that she could reach Atlas, get closer, stroke his cheek. But he was so high up – he was high above her head, stuck on his archway, and the girl could not even reach his feet. She would never be able to touch him, even if she grew to be ten feet tall. All she could do was talk to Atlas, stand beneath him, witness his pain.

'"I hope you know that I am here," she would say. "I am just a small girl, but I see you. You are not alone."

'Atlas would never answer.

'Then one day, the girl realised she had stayed too long in the garden and it was suddenly dark. She had to get home before her mama became worried. So she ran from the gate, ran as fast as she could, along the cobbled laneway and out onto the road. And at that very moment, a horse and cart were racing down the road, racing right towards the girl in the dark. She stood frozen, unable to move. It seemed that she would be crushed right there, killed, and her mama would be sad for the rest of her days. Sad and all alone.

'But just as the horse and cart were right on her, someone pulled her out of the way. It was Atlas. He had thrown the heavens from his shoulders and had leapt down from his arch. He'd taken three giant steps and snatched the small girl up in his arms. The horse and cart sped past, missing the girl by a whisker. A moment.

'Atlas had come to life.

'He looked down at the girl, his only friend in the whole city. The only one who saw him. And the girl reached up and stroked his cheek. She was finally able to touch her giant.

'Atlas shed a tear.

'He put the girl down safely on the pavement. He bowed to her, then he turned and picked up the celestial sphere. He climbed up to his place on the arch and became frozen once more. A stone Titan carrying the sky and the heavens on his shoulders for all of time.

'The girl ran home and told her mama that Atlas had saved her life. And from that day on, the girl and her mama left flowers at the gate for Atlas, to say thank you and to remind him that he was not alone.'

Aunty Máňa stopped talking then. Luděk could hear her heavy breath. He stayed still. Was that the end of the story? He wanted there to be more. What happened when the girl grew up? Did Atlas ever come to life again? Is he still holding up the sky?

Luděk sat up.

'Was that girl you?' he asked.

He could see Aunty start to smile. She gently pushed him back and he lay down again against his pillow.

'The story is not over,' she said.

'When Atlas threw the sphere off his shoulders to save the girl, it left a big crater in the stone pathway below the arch. That crater is still there today. When it rains, the crater fills up with clean water from the heavens. It is said that when a bird drinks from that water, it can sing and understand all the songs of this world.

'It is also said that if a man drinks from the water, he will understand all the stories and all the languages of this world.'

'Where is it? Where is Atlas?' Luděk asked.

Aunty Máňa smiled. 'Time for sleep now,' she said.

'Was the girl you?' Luděk asked again. He looked at her face, looked right in her eyes. They stayed perfectly still. She never gave anything away, just like Babi.

She kissed him on the forehead and turned off the lamp.

'How will I find Atlas if you don't tell me where he is?' Luděk said.

He heard the floorboards creak under her feet as she walked to the door.

'You will find him one day,' she said. 'Now go to sleep.'

Then she was gone.

The bed was warm now, almost too hot. Luděk turned over and listened to the adults talking. He could make out no words, just the hum of voices. It was nice to have voices in the flat. Real voices, and not just the television telling you this and telling you that. It was nice for Babi to have people to talk to every night. Friends. Family. Her sister. Máňa and Eva. Eva and Máňa. With a white streak like lightning in their hair.

Uncle Bill and Aunty Máňa would be gone tomorrow, and they would not come back for a very long time. They lived far away and they had to save the money to come again. They would not come back for three years, maybe four, and Luděk would be old by then. He would be far too old for bedtime stories. He would be far too old for Atlas.

He fell asleep to the song of voices singing softly about the past, and about the present, voices that were too scared to make any plans for any future because they knew they had no power over it. They knew they had no power over anything.

The flat was quiet when he woke. It was late. He'd been in a total blackout, falling through nothing. The last thing he remembered was Aunty Máňa standing in the doorway, the shape of her there, saying goodnight – saying goodbye. After so long here, Aunty Máňa and Uncle Bill were gone.

The flat felt too big. The flat felt empty.

Babi was in the kitchen smoking. There was no radio, no music, and her face was a solid slab of concrete. Her eyes found his, but she was unreadable.

She got up from the table and started to cut some bread. His breakfast – sliced bread, butter, a glass of water. Luděk sat down at the table and Babi put the food down in front of him. Still, she did not speak.

He ate his breakfast. He drank down his water. He looked out of the window and the light was grey. It still felt warm but maybe it would rain today. It probably would rain. He got up and put his plate and glass in the sink, and he wished he could make time run backwards. He wished he could press rewind.

Rewind. Stop. Play.

Luděk ran out of the kitchen and into the hall. He skidded into his bedroom and pulled open his top drawer. He had not played it for ages – Mama's cassette tape, the one she had made just for him.

The old radio-cassette player sat on the kitchen windowsill. It was the spot with the best reception. Sometimes they even picked up radio programs from West Germany or from Poland. Not often. Not often enough. Mostly the radio was just endless talking, endless romantic duets, endless nothing.

Luděk shoved the cassette into the slot and pushed it shut. He pressed the play button down hard, and the wheels began to run.

A low hum.

A pause.

Luděk turned the volume up, and it began.

The strange plucked melody, bending and curving and swirling out of the speakers. Then a drumbeat stomping down.

Bang, bang, bang, bang, bang, bang, bang, bang.

The beat was hypnotic, it marched on, and when the song smashed open with cymbals, Luděk started to move. He kicked out his legs, each foot flying up with the beat.

'Someone will hear!' Babi said and she moved towards the cassette player, but Luděk blocked her – he kicked out harder. He kicked out higher.

Bang, bang, bang, bang, bang, bang, bang, crash!

'Luděk, you will break something!' she said.

But Luděk didn't care. He kept on dancing, the song more frantic, more driving, and he spun in circles now – around and around with the droning bass, his limbs flying free. One of his slippers flew off and hit the wall. The other skidded out on the wooden floorboards in the hall. Luděk spun again, barefoot now.

It was Mama's favourite song. 'Paint it Black'.

He did not understand the words, the singing. But he knew what the song felt like, how it was urgent and alive and crazy. It pulled you right up out of yourself. It shot you into the sky.

Luděk grabbed Babi's hands. He swung her big arms side to side with all of his force, and finally her feet started to step to the beat. Step, tap, step, tap. Bang, crash, bang, crash!

He moved with her. His face was hot and there was sweat down his back, but he couldn't stop now. Babi's head was shaking, and her body was swaying, her arms rocking to the beat, and she was dancing. She was really dancing.

The song went on and on in a loop of endless rhythm until it eventually faded out. Babi was panting and breathless. 'Enough now,' she said.

Luděk pressed stop before the next song started up. Babi stood by the window and took some deep breaths, her hands on her hips.

'Where did this music come from?' she said, and she took another big gulp of air.

'It's Mama's,' Luděk said.

Babi shook her head. Her daughter – always in trouble. Always the rebel.

'Downstairs will complain,' she said. But her face was alive and shiny, the corners of her mouth smiling. 'You dance crazy, like your grandfather.' And she let out a sharp laugh, some snap of memory.

There was nothing better than when Babi laughed. Sometimes Luděk would hear her from his bedroom, laughing at one of the comedy shows she liked on TV. A sudden bolt of laughter she could no longer hold in. Uncontrolled. Uncensored. Real.

She pulled out a chair and sat down at the kitchen table.

'Go and wash up!' she said. 'Get dressed.' She waved him off, picked up her cigarettes.

She was back.

Alena

Rock and roll flies out of his portable radio like an electrical storm.

Signals from the other side – sounds that she has never heard.

'I told you I could get reception,' Tomáš says, and he is smiling at her. 'I listen every night. It's all I think about.'

Now she will think about it, too. The feeling of the music – the beat – the drive. Freedom. And she wants to move, to dance. She drains her wine, takes Tomáš's hand.

They dance to the Beatles; they dance to Jimi Hendrix. They dance to the static that comes when they lose the signal.

Tomáš. This tall man – a writer, so vibrant and alive.

And maybe everything *is* going to be different now – this spring of hope, this wave of change.

They dance to the Rolling Stones. And outside it rains. She can finally breathe.

Melbourne

1980

My grandpa is fixing Uncle Joe's car.

It's a bright purple Ford Falcon and it takes forever to warm up. The engine rumbles low and fat and rocks my whole frame when it starts. It is *a beast*. It is too big to fit in my grandpa's small garage, so he has to work on it in the driveway.

My grandpa can make any engine part he needs on his metal lathe. He was a toolmaker for over thirty years in London and I thought that meant he made tools like hammers and screwdrivers and wrenches, but he told me it meant that he made *parts* for things, like parts for clocks and speedometers. The insides of moving machines.

'It is all maths,' he told me, 'angles, degrees, *precision*.'

He could even make a cog in a watch, tiny and perfect. The part that kept time moving.

'My son knows nothing about cars,' my grandpa says, his

white singlet already smeared with grease. It's on his skin, too, on his arms – a small smudge of it on his forehead.

'Plenty of work in Australia, he said. I don't know why we listened.'

My grandpa has taken his watch off, and I get to look after it. The band is too big for me. Even when I secure it on the last hole, the one closest to the face, it still slips right off my wrist. I just hold it carefully in my hand.

Uncle Joe says my grandpa should get a new watch, a digital one like his that lights up green when you press a button. But my grandpa does not want a digital watch. He likes his watch.

'You can take it inside,' my grandpa says. But I shake my head. I like to hold it, to look at the face. It's gold, real gold, and the band is soft and worn. The second hand speeds around so quickly, racing on and on.

My grandpa opened it up to show me once. The insides. He took it apart piece by piece, cog by cog, tiny spring by tiny spring. Then, with his special glasses on, he put it all back together again. He set the spring and – like magic – the watch began to tick, to move – alive.

What should the working day be made of? My grandpa asked.
  Eight hours for work.
  Eight hours for sleep.
  Eight hours for family, I answered.
  The eight-hour day.

My grandpa loved the workers. He loved classical music and smoking his pipe. He loved my grandma's cooking and playing cards, especially cribbage. Those are the things he loved.

There were only a few things that my grandpa hated. He hated having his feet tickled when he was almost asleep. He hated it when anyone crunched their food loudly, especially things like potato chips or raw carrots. He hated swimming and he did not like to fly.

———⚡———

They had been away for six long weeks, but now they were back – finally home. My grandpa was tired and my grandma was quiet. She sat in her chair, not watching TV, not really looking at anything.

'How was staying with Uncle Joe?' my grandpa asked.

'We got McDonald's,' I said.

My grandpa smiled. 'I guess that's better than having to eat Uncle Joe's cooking,' he said.

They bought me a Czechoslovakian doll in traditional dress, with puffy white sleeves and embroidered patterns on her skirt – red and green and yellow. Black boots made of felt, a crown of white flowers in her hair. Her eyes closed when you laid her down and opened when you stood her up, and she had rosy, bright cheeks. Her name was Kateřina. It said that on the box.

'Your grandma chose that,' my grandpa said.

He did not care for dolls, and when my grandma was asleep in her chair, my grandpa gave me a small black box. Inside was a glass swan swimming on velvet. My grandpa told me that it was not normal glass but crystal, and that when he had seen it in a shop he had thought of me. The swan had its head resting down against its chest like it was sleeping, its long neck curled, and when I held it up to the light it caught all the colours and held them inside each feather of its graceful body.

'Thank you,' I said, and I hugged my grandpa, and his cheek was warm and rough with stubble.

Uncle Joe gave my grandpa a silver Beta video recorder and three blank tapes to say thank you for fixing his car.

'It probably fell off the back of a truck,' my grandpa said, and he raised his eyebrows at me. He carefully read the instruction manual, and he practised recording small snippets of TV until he had the hang of it.

The first important thing my grandma made him tape was the Sunday afternoon movie, *Doctor Zhivago*.

'Don't miss the start,' she said and my grandpa waved her off. He pressed record as the music started up – the heavy drums, and the marching chants, the orchestra, and finally the melody of the balalaika.

At the first ad break, my grandpa paused the recording. My grandma was very pleased about this, it meant there would be no ads when we watched the video. It would be like a proper film, with no breaks, no talking, no distractions. But my grandpa said that there was no way he was going to sit there and watch the *whole bloody thing*. He really hated *Doctor Zhivago*.

'How many times can you watch this rubbish?' he asked.

But my grandma really loved *Doctor Zhivago*. I had to watch it with her many times. It was very long and it seemed very complicated to me – I could never follow the story. Endless fields of wheat, soldiers marching, snow forever, and the grey-black cold. I would fall asleep somewhere in those endless fields, and suddenly wake up to the Tuckerbag puppet yelling in his squeaky voice about ham, or a Stan Cash ad, a Southern Motors ad, or a song about *hot stuff* – Four'n Twenty pies.

'Why couldn't he just stay and stop all the ads?' my grandma would say. And the movie would start up again and we would be thrust back into Russia, a different scene, a different season – maybe on a train pushing through snow, a hundred starving faces packed together in a carriage like cattle.

But the part of the movie I remember most is the beginning.

A small boy stands by a grave dug out of the cold earth. An open coffin is carried out – a beautiful woman lying inside, white lace around her head and face. Autumn leaves start to fall from the sky and the boy looks up. He watches the leaves. The coffin lid is put on and nailed shut with many long nails.

The leaves keep on falling. Hard, frozen soil is dropped on the coffin until the hole is filled. The boy walks over and puts flowers at the head of the grave. But the wind picks up, a snowstorm is coming. Everyone rushes from the grave and the boy is dragged along with them. There is only the grave now, and the snow and the howling wind. And the little boy's flowers get blown away.

She was strong, my grandma, and when I lay in the bed next to her large body, I felt safe. I slept so well. There were no dreams, no nightmares – and I never even thought about my parents at all, and I did not need them – just the soft ticking of the Smiths clock and my grandma's breathing. Nothing could touch me when I was with her in that room. But that sound of the balalaika made my grandma cry every time. *Doctor Zhivago.*

She must have watched that movie twenty times or more.

By Christmas, all three of the videotapes had movies recorded on them. One was *Doctor Zhivago*, one was *The Return of the Pink Panther*, which made my grandpa laugh, and the last one was *Willy Wonka and the Chocolate Factory*. My grandpa recorded it for me and every single ad was gone. He had sat through the whole thing and paused the recorder so that I could put the tape on and stay in that world of pure imagination, and not get pulled out by anything.

I clutch the program tightly to my chest. My grandma pushes me forward to the very front row, and when I look up to the domed ceiling, I am blinded by the lights that hang down, by the balconies shining like gold.

People sit down around me. There is the hum of voices, the hum of movement, but soon a hush comes down.

'You must be quiet now,' my grandma whispers.

Yes, I nod. Quiet now.

The lights go out.

My eyes burn wide in the dark.

I reach for my grandma's arm and she takes my hand, squeezes it tight. She keeps hold of it.

Music begins – a violin's soft call reaches out and fills the space. I can almost see it there, the shape of it moving. It keeps playing, and the sound rises all the way to the sky. The curtain opens.

Colours in the darkness. Pink and green and yellow fluorescent.

Hallucinations of bright light.

A week of stories.

A week of dreams.

A giant spider, an electric pig. A pair of trousers that dance alive on the washing line. A suitcase with yellow eyes – a suitcase with a mouth like a big black hole.

I was lost to the stories, to the creatures. I was lost in the dream, but the lights came on, bright like the sun, and the theatre erupted in noise, in applause. I stood up and clapped until my hands stung. Humans walked out onto the stage and took a graceful bow, all in a line. A dancer's bow. Flowers were thrown, red and pink, and a woman with long blonde hair picked them up. She waved, blew a kiss to the audience. She was beautiful. I knew she had played the mermaid in the show, the mermaid who had visited a man as he slept. He had left the tap on before he went to bed, and his room had slowly filled with water. The mermaid swam around the room, swam above his bed and her long hair hung down and touched the skin on his sleeping face. But he did not wake. He stayed dreaming.

The clapping rose again as three more humans came out onto the stage. They were dressed completely in black, even their faces were covered. They peeled off their masks and they bowed and one of them was Alena. I clapped even harder. Even louder.

Alena – one of the invisible people. One of the ghosts that made all the objects move, made the magic real.

Backstage.

I got to stand with the dancers, to be near them, and they gave me apple juice and there were chocolates and my grandma even had a glass of champagne. Everyone was speaking Czech. I listened to the words floating above my head, felt the patterns they made. I heard the song, but I did not understand it.

There was a man in a white shirt standing on his own, and I could not stop staring at him, at his dark eyes and his sharp face. He was staring at me, too. He walked over, and he reached down and put a hand on my head.

'You *must* join the theatre,' he said, and his accent was strong and commanding and he did not smile.

I blinked and blinked, and his hand felt heavy on my head. He wasn't tall, he wasn't big, but I knew this man was The Magician. They were his dreams I had been watching. It was his theatre.

Someone squeezed my shoulder. My grandma. 'Say thank you to Mr Srnec,' she said.

'Jiří,' he said.

'Thank you,' I said. And he still did not smile.

'I will be waiting for you,' he said, and he lifted his hand off my head. 'You must come.'

Alena was suddenly there with her shiny black hair and she said, 'Yes! You must come. You must come because I need to hug you.'

She grabbed me up and squeezed me into her. She felt so warm in her black velvet jumpsuit and her long hair fell all over my face.

'I will hug you and I will not let you go.'

I listened to her speak Czech with my grandma, another song, another shape floating out into space. My grandma was smiling and she kissed Alena on the cheek and then she told me to be good – *be a good girl* – and somehow it was decided.

I *was* going.

The Victoria Hotel.

Alena said I could call her aunty. She wasn't really my aunty because my grandmother was *her* aunty. She held my hand. The Magician walked ahead, he walked alone and he didn't speak until we stepped through the glass doors of the hotel and into the foyer and stood under the huge glass chandelier. Then he said goodnight. I watched him move up the curved staircase like he was floating, like he weighed nothing at all. Then he was gone.

Some of the dancers headed towards the hotel bar. They were still wide awake – terribly awake and alive.

'Is it sleep time for Little Fox?' they said to me, and they waved goodbye. I wanted to stay awake with them, I wanted to stay, but my eyes blurred like they were trying to close.

'Sleep tight,' a man called Aleš said to me. Aleš with his dark beard. He kissed me on the cheek.

Alena led me up the curved stairs, then down a very long corridor that went on forever and ever. Her room was small – a chair, a bed, a darkened window. The curtains were open but no light came through the glass.

She put me to bed and sang a song from a place far away. I lay in the warm bed and my eyes started to close.

'Luděk,' I heard her say.

And maybe she was crying. But my eyes were heavy. I tumbled into sleep. I tumbled into dreams.

I tumble through space. I see Neptune, blue and brilliant, and then I see the sun. I fall towards Earth and land on the back of a white swan that carries me above an old city covered with snow. There are stone towers, and stone bridges over a long, curving river. I see a small boy running the streets, running and running, and I want to run with him, I want to call out, *Wait for me*. But then I am alone in a room, empty and bare, except for an old suitcase. It's the suitcase with yellow eyes. *Don't open it – don't look inside*. But its mouth opens wide, and I tumble – I fall into endless black.

I wake, and it's light. Alena is dressed and she is sitting in the chair, her face turned towards the window that looks out onto a laneway. Her eyes are lost, unfocused. But then they find me. She smiles.

'Hello,' she says. 'Time for breakfast.'

Alena drinks black coffee and she watches me eat. The toast and the eggs and the baked beans and the bowl of canned fruit salad. It is the *good* fruit salad, the one that has bright-red, squeaky cherries in it. There are two cherries in my bowl. I spoon up the sweet syrup and drink it down.

'Eat! Eat!' Alena says. 'Have some more.'

'Yes – eat!' It is Aleš and he sits down at our table. He only has toast on his plate, a cup of black coffee in his hand. He looks very tired, his eyes sunk right down into the deep hollows above his cheekbones. His hair hangs limp.

The Magician is not in the breakfast room. I look for him. I keep my eyes on the door, but he never comes through. I see the other dancers – I see the mermaid and the man who flew on the bicycle. I see the man who left the tap on while he slept. But I do not see The Magician.

Aleš's cup of coffee is empty now. He looks at Alena. He rests his big hands on the table but then one of them moves to Alena's shoulder, just gently, just touching, and he smiles at her. She shakes her head slowly, and her eyes move towards the door. Aleš follows her eyes with his, and he lifts his hand from her shoulder. He moves it to his empty cup. I turn and see a man walk from the door to an empty table. He sits down. He is wearing shiny metal glasses and a dark-blue tie. He opens the newspaper but he's not really looking at it – his eyes move around the room, from table to table. He watches.

I turn back to Aleš.

'Our beloved manager,' Aleš whispers, and he winks at me.

Alena leans forward, her elbow on the table, and her delicate hand covers her mouth. But her eyes smile. I can see that. Her eyes almost laugh. They look at Aleš.

My grandpa was there to pick me up suddenly, tall and booming in his dark-blue night watchman uniform. He looked tired and I held his hand as we walked to the car.

We drove out of the city, on the big busy roads, and I told my grandpa about the breakfast at the hotel – about the trays of sausages and scrambled eggs, the trays of baked beans, roasted tomatoes, fried bacon. The piles of toast, the butter, the jam. The fruit salad.

'How lucky,' he said.

Back at the flat, I watched my grandpa eat his breakfast, his bread and dripping, his hardboiled egg, and he winked at me. He knew I hated dripping, even the smell of it, but he could not do without it. He said it was from all those years in London, because even after the war rationing went on and on, and there was never any butter, only dripping, and he got so used to it that now he loved it. When he made himself sausages in the heavy black frypan, he wouldn't wash up. He'd leave the pan there on the stove, and later there would be white fat congealed like a pond that froze in the night, and he would scrape it up and put it in a china dish and spread it on his toast and that was dripping.

My grandpa was always happy when he was eating food. Maybe he liked it more than anything else. Maybe he wished that there was more on his plate, more in the cupboard, more in his wallet. Maybe he wished he could say, *Let's go out for lunch, Let's go out for dinner, Let's go and get some cake.* But my grandpa had to be careful with money and that was how it was. It was everything, and it held us together like packing tape on a cardboard box. But one day I hoped that I could take my grandpa to a hotel so that he could eat as many sausages and as much bacon as he wanted. Just one time. I knew that's what I would do if I had lots of money. I'd take my grandpa to a hotel buffet breakfast and watch him eat until he could eat no more.

We went to the theatre two more times, and even though it was the same show, I was never bored. There was more and more inside each dream, more inside each story.

I stood with Alena backstage in her black velvet jumpsuit and she talked to me half in her language and half in mine. Somehow I understood it all: her life at home, her son – a small boy called Luděk who liked to run. She told me that before things had been not so good, and that the days and nights had rolled together like one.

'My husband died,' she squeezed my hand, closed her eyes. 'He was so young.'

Alena bent down, whispered in my ear, 'I'm going to try to stay here.'

I wanted to ask her what she meant, but it was time to go. My grandma wouldn't let me stay at the hotel again.

'Alena needs to rest,' my grandma said.

I waved goodbye.

'See you on Sunday,' she said.

Sunday. Three days away.

In the car, on the way home, I asked my grandma if Alena was coming to live with us. She was quiet, her face still. No one said anything.

'Is Luděk coming, too?' I asked.

My grandpa cleared his throat. 'It's nothing for you to worry about,' he said.

But later, when he came to tuck me into the big double bed, he told me that if Alena stayed here then no other family would be able to leave Czechoslovakia, not even her son. He spoke quietly.

'It's like a guarantee,' he said. 'They only let her come on tour because her son stays there, her mother stays there, her brother. You see?' I nodded, but I didn't really understand.

'Will she stay?' I said, and I wanted her to stay. I wanted her to live with us.

'It's very complicated,' my grandpa said, and he let out a long sigh.

I knew my grandpa loved Czechoslovakia, that he missed it, that he looked forward to going there. So wasn't it a good place?

'It is home,' he said, 'but there is not much freedom. There is food, clothes, electricity, but no dreams. That is very hard for some people. That can make you go crazy.'

'Will she have to leave her son?' I said, and my grandpa sniffed.

'It's very complicated,' he said.

He tucked me in even tighter, so tightly I could hardly move.

'Nothing is *all* good or *all* bad,' he said. 'There are problems everywhere.'

I knew my grandpa was talking about the workers – about unemployment and interest rates and the rent going up again. I knew he was worried that they would have to move to a smaller flat with only one bedroom. Somewhere without a garage workshop. I did not want to think about them losing the flat, their home, and I could feel myself falling asleep. The doona was warm, my eyes heavy, and maybe I was already asleep. Maybe I was dreaming, but I could hear my grandpa's voice, just softly.

'It is easy to think somewhere else is better. But when you leave home, there are things you miss that you never imagined you would. Small things. Like the smell of the river, or the sound of rain on the cobblestones, the taste of local beer. You long to have those things again – to see them, to smell them – and when you do, you know that you are home.'

My grandpa told me that Pavel, the man with the shiny metal glasses, was a spy.

And maybe that's why the rest of the theatre did not wake him when he fell asleep in the sun. They left him there for hours and he got cooked, pink like ham.

It wasn't even hot – it was only spring – but still the sun was strong enough to burn and strong enough for me to run into the sea and run out again, and for Alena and Aleš to run in with me. Even my grandma put her feet in the water.

Elwood Beach – with the skyscrapers of the city in view.

My grandpa and Pavel were the only two people who didn't swim, or even wade, in the water. My grandpa because he never, ever swam or even put his feet near the water. And Pavel because he fell asleep on a towel on the sand almost as soon as we all got to the beach. And he stayed like that until it was time to leave. Then he didn't feel so good. He had a headache and he had to go back to the Victoria Hotel, and a doctor was called. The doctor said he had sunstroke and he had to spend the night in hospital.

Everyone was so pleased by this news.

It was Sunday. There could be a night off away from those shiny metal glasses and those ice-blue eyes – watching, watching, always watching.

'Cheers to our good old manager, Pavel,' Aleš said and he winked at me. He lifted up his glass of wine. *'Na zdraví.'* Cheers.

A night off – to drink, to share food, to laugh and dance. They were all at our place, filling up the third storey flat – even The Magician.

A feast.

Bottles of beer and bottles of wine – lemonade for me, sweet and fizzy. Chicken schnitzels, fried potato, cucumber salad.

That was my favourite – cucumber salad with cream and vinegar and black pepper, chilled from the fridge so all the cucumber juice got sucked out of the cucumber slices and mixed in with the cream. The salad bowl still had some of the cream left in the bottom and I couldn't stop staring at it. I wanted to grab the big bowl up in my hands and drink the cream down.

The Magician leaned into me, whispered in my ear. 'I want to drink the cream, too,' he said. 'I love cucumber salad.'

My face felt hot.

And then he stood up, raised a glass to my grandma. The room fell silent.

'What wonderful food,' he said. 'Thank you, Máňa. It's so nice to feel like we are home. We have all been away for too long.'

Everyone clapped. Everybody drank. Home.

My grandma's cheeks were red, and maybe it was from all the little drinks that kept being poured and drunk quickly, or from all the laughter, or because there was not one scrap left on anyone's plate. The food had been devoured.

My grandma was a good cook.

I took all the plates and bowls and cutlery into the small kitchen by myself. I wanted to do it and it took me a long time. There were so many plates and dishes, more than ever before, and I had to stack them up on the kitchen table because they did not all fit on the sink top.

My grandpa came in to get more beer from the fridge. 'Leave that,' he said, and he had a spring in his step. 'We can wash up tomorrow.'

My grandma put a marble cake and biscuits on the dining table and there was only Czech in the room. Shapes and colours like smoke. And sometimes I understood every single word like it was there in my blood, there in my bones, and sometimes I understood nothing at all but laughter and bright eyes.

Alena pushed her chair in next to mine, and she grabbed my hand under the table, squeezed it tight.

'This flat is so much like my mother's flat,' she said. 'It even smells the same. It's so strange! I think your grandmother never left home.'

Aleš looked at us from across the table. He did not laugh like everyone else. He drank, he smoked, he stared at Alena but she would not look at him. She just kept on squeezing my hand.

'Have some biscuits, some cake,' she said, and when I looked over at my grandma she nodded a happy yes. I took one of the hazelnut crescent biscuits and it crumbled in my mouth – rich and good. More drinking, music playing on the stereo, and my grandma's face was shiny and full like the moon.

Alena got up from the table and walked out of the room. Aleš followed her with his eyes. He lit a cigarette. I took another biscuit, one of the jam-filled ones with icing sugar on top, and scoffed it down. People were starting to move into the lounge and someone turned the stereo up. A different tape, a different sound. The Rolling Stones – swirling electric.

I want to follow the music, the beat, but I walk down the hall.

Alena.

I see her at the phone table in the dark, her head against the wall.

She sits there, the receiver in her hand, the receiver to her ear.

Not speaking.

Not listening.

The phone is dead – cut off. There is no one on the other side.

Still she holds the receiver.

'Luděk,' she says, softly.

I step closer. 'It's me,' I say.

'It's you,' she says, her dark eyes on mine. She reaches for my hand.

'I want to stay,' she says, and I blink my eyes – once, twice. 'But I just can't.'

She pulls me into her, holds me tightly. I can feel her breath on the top of my head. We stay like that.

The music gets louder.

'I'm going to have a baby,' she says.

The door to the lounge opens like an explosion of light, of sound – a beat stomping down.

'Little Fox! Little Fox!' Someone yells, and I'm pulled into the room. The dancers surround me, free and wild – spinning, jumping – the bass sliding in-out, in-out. Even my grandma and grandpa are dancing slowly together. Suddenly my grandma lets loose with the beat. She kicks off her shoes and moves in her stockinged feet. Everyone follows and kicks off their shoes, and one shoe nearly hits my grandpa in the face. The room is packed. The room is full of life. Shoes in the corners, furniture pushed to the walls, bare feet dancing. My grandma's beehive shakes itself loose and her long hair falls. The white streak shines.

I dance with everyone. I even dance with The Magician and he holds my hands and swings me into the air and round and round. I am dizzy with it. I am free. And if the lady downstairs is banging her broomstick on her ceiling in complaint as she likes to do, then no one can hear it. Even when the song fades out in an endless loop, the laughter and panting and clapping drown out the stillness and the ticking clock.

I see Alena on the other side of the room. Aleš stands near and they are talking. Alena keeps shaking her head, her hands by her sides.

A new song starts – slower but still rocking, with a real swing. The dancers around me start to clap along with the sharp claps on the recording. They know this song by heart. They sing along. 'Under My Thumb'.

Aleš reaches for Alena's arm, but she pulls away. He reaches again, again, and finally she lets him touch her. He pulls her towards him and she falls into his tall frame. He holds her close like he's saying, *I know. It's okay.* There are no words, just the beat and bodies moving, messages flying like bright ribbons across the room from adult to adult. And I am underneath it all.

I'm spinning, spinning – suddenly so sleepy.

I sit down on the couch and my eyes are heavy, and the smoke haze in the room gets thicker. The music keeps playing but it is muffled now, and Alena kisses me on the cheek, but then she changes shape, she turns into The Magician.

'I will see you again in a few years. It is not so long. Just a week of dreams,' he says.

And I wake up in bed with my grandma sleeping beside me. The theatre has gone.

The flat feels too big. The flat feels empty. I can hear my grandpa snoring.

All that is left of the magic is the tape in the cassette player – a tape alive with rock and roll. Alive with the Rolling Stones.

When the telephone rang in the hallway of that third storey flat, it was always someone we knew, or something important – like the bank, or the travel agent or the state electricity commission. The telephone did not ring often, but when it did my grandma would panic. She had no confidence speaking on the phone, and even though it was usually family, sometimes even her sister calling from Prague, my grandma always made my grandpa answer it. She would stand behind him, hover there, while my grandpa picked up the receiver.

'Hello, William Kopek speaking,' he would say in an English accent, like a man from the BBC news, and not my grandpa at all. My grandpa could hide all traces of his real accent when he wanted to.

'Who is it?' My grandma would ask, her ear as close to the receiver as she could get it. My grandpa would wave her off.

'Yes, I understand. I believe that account has been paid. Thank you for the call.'

My grandpa would hang up the phone, stand and rub his forehead.

The bills lived in a pile on the dining table. We only used the dining table on special occasions, and my grandpa would write letters, do the crossword, or pay the bills sitting at the dining table. Bills would always be paid at the very last minute. My grandpa would write a cheque on the due date, and not before. He figured it was better to get the tiny amount of interest on his savings than give these companies the chance to do the same and make more money.

My grandpa had very good handwriting. He said it was because of his job, that technical drawing taught you precise lettering. His writing was very clear and ordered – with every capital letter coming out the exact same height and width. But he could also write in a beautiful curly copperplate when he wanted to, and he would always write like that on Christmas cards, and birthday cards, and letters. He said that kind of writing came from a long time ago, from school, only it was not in English but in Czech, so he had to practise it with English for many years.

Dear Little Fox,
Merry Christmas
Bless your little head, Bill x

If my grandpa wasn't home, my grandma dreaded the telephone ringing. The sound of it would make her jump, and she would stand in the hall, frozen still.

Sometimes she wouldn't answer it at all. We would just stand there together and the phone would ring and ring, and it felt like it would never end.

But sometimes she would reach out, pick up the heavy green receiver.

'Hello?' A question. Her soft, quiet voice.

Relief. Her eyes smiling. An explosion of Czech, fast and running altogether. It was her sister, her son, a friend. It was okay.

I'm marching. I'm a soldier marching off to war. The *1812 Overture*.

I turn, stride back along the lounge room as the music gets loud and excited with brass and crashing.

I look at my grandpa sitting in his armchair. 'Were you a soldier?' I ask.

The music softens, and the swirling strings begin.

My grandpa never talked about the war. But it was there in the way he walked, in the way he sometimes could not sleep.

'I wanted to fight,' he said, and he filled his pipe, lit it carefully and puffed in quick succession – *puff-puff-puff.* I could see the tobacco burn orange as my grandpa inhaled.

'I wanted to fight, but I had to stay.'

At first, he could only get a job on the factory floor working with watches and clocks. Then someone realised he had trained as a toolmaker, and that he was very good at this. Soon he was head toolmaker. Soon he had his own team.

Suddenly, even though he was a foreigner, he got to work on very exciting things. Important things to do with aeroplanes. Important things to do with winning the war.

'We had to fight from the Smiths Factory and from Hendon Aerodrome,' he said, and he blinked then, my grandpa – maybe thinking of the factory, or about aeroplane controls, about London, a place he spent thirty-two years of his life living and working and raising a family.

He puffed on his pipe.

'That's when I started to smoke a pipe,' he said. And he took his pipe out of his mouth, held it in his hand. He nodded his head.

'At Smiths, everyone was always asking, *Hey, Billy, give us a cigarette*. Cheeky sods.' He puffed again.

'So I gave up the cigarettes. I started to smoke a pipe.'

He was smiling now. 'No one ever asked if they could have a puff.'

I sat on my stool, the big one, and kicked my legs out. I wanted to play cards but we would not play until my grandpa had finished his pipe.

The overture was getting loud again and soon the cannons would come.

'We lived right near Hendon Aerodrome,' my grandpa said, 'so I could walk to work. And I could even go home for a hot lunch. That was good. I liked to do that, and it was a nice flat. We made the best of it even with all the bombs. We tried to make it a home. But then someone decided that foreigners couldn't live near Hendon Aerodrome. Maybe they thought your grandma was a spy.'

My grandpa paused then, looked into the distance.

'But guess what?'

I shrugged. I could not guess.

'The flat they moved us to was only eight hundred metres away from the one we had.'

My grandpa let out a single laugh then. 'Ha! Did they think a spy could not walk the extra eight hundred metres to the aerodrome?'

He puffed on his pipe, but it was out of tobacco. It was burnt out. He tapped the black contents into the ashtray and put his pipe down on the ceramic plate holder next to his chair.

My grandpa looked at me then, right in my eyes.

'Lots of rules are pointless,' he said. 'You don't have to follow everything. Make your own mind up about what is right.'

I nodded. I picked up the pack of cards as the church bells rang and tumbled and the cannons fired in victory.

Vilém

The shelter is crowded. Maybe it's another false alarm, but the air raid siren just keeps on screaming. It won't rest.

'It's okay,' he says softly to Máňa. He speaks in English.

There are a few men in the shelter who he works with. Neighbours. He recognises them in the yellow glow of torchlight. They only speak to him at work. In the street, they might make eye contact and sometimes they even nod, but that is it. There is never a smile, never a polite question asked about the day, about the weather, about family. No questions. No handshake. He is not one of them.

But he understands. He has heard it all so many times before.

'He's all right I suppose, but that one, that *Marie* or whatever she calls herself – hardly any bloody English for a start. I don't care what they keep saying about Czechoslovakia. They could be Germans for all we know.'

He can feel Máňa shiver now and he holds her tighter. It terrifies him to think that he might not have met her, that he might have missed it. This one good thing in his life.

At home, alone in their flat, they are happy. Work is fine and Máňa is relieved they finally have their own place. But she must practise more English.

She tries. She listens to the radio all day and she understands every single word that is said. But her accent – it is stubborn. It does not want to leave. Maybe she can't let it go because it is the one thing she still has from home. The one thing that totally belongs to her.

There is crying from somewhere in the shadows. A woman crying. Everyone is waiting for the big explosion that will blow up Hendon Aerodrome. Everyone is waiting in this shelter to die.

He touches Máňa's face, runs his fingers along one cheekbone. He loves her face – her strong face. *They* talk about her face, the women in the street. About how it is so different. *So foreign. So strange.*

Sometimes he wants to yell out that they have boring, flat faces that no one will ever remember or stare at or even notice at all. But he never yells out anything. He keeps quiet. He is polite. He gets on with his work and is grateful for that.

Anyway, none of these people matter now because they have to move again. All foreigners are to be moved away from Hendon Aerodrome. A year ago, they were moved so he could be *close* to Hendon Aerodrome and the factory.

He does not know where they will live now, he only knows they have to pack and be ready. More neighbours that will hate them, hate their height and their cheekbones and their names and their accents.

Máňa must work on her accent. She looks up at him.

Vilém, she mouths silently.

Nobody knows his real name.

He had practised this new one, saying it over and over, *Wwwilliam. Wwwilliam.* He had concentrated on the strange sound of W, witnessed how it made his mouth move in the bathroom mirror. *Wwwilliam.*

He couldn't be Vilém anymore. He had to leave Vilém behind. And maybe the shadow of Vilém was still there, lying in the bed by the window high on the third floor, above the narrow, cobbled street, listening to his little brother sleep through the night.

But he may as well not have practised his Ws at all, because on his first day of work everyone just called him Bill.

Bill, Billy, Billy-Boy. Tall old Bill. Sometimes Will – but never William, and never, ever Vilém.

He must be Bill.

The sirens fade. The all clear rings out at long last. He takes a long breath.

The only way to live now is to keep moving and not look back. It is the only way his heart can keep on beating and not break. He must look forward – and never behind.

He must never look behind.

Prague
1980

Ludĕk had tried to find Atlas. He'd spent a whole month of Saturdays trying, but it was no use. He didn't even know who to ask. He could not ask Babi because then she would know he was running around town, instead of playing at the park like she thought – playing with the other kids in the street. But he hated their games. The other kids were all so boring. Maybe Atlas was made up? Maybe the statue didn't even exist, because he had looked everywhere – in all the little gardens he knew, in all the public squares around. Nothing.

He walked into the kitchen. Babi was reading her magazine and smoking a cigarette. On the cover were three women doing some kind of exercise routine. They were all blonde. It was always the same story, the same kind of picture. It was always sunny on the cover of *Kvĕty* magazine.

Why couldn't he just forget Atlas? Why couldn't he just think about something else?

'Babi? he said. 'Old Lady Bla . . . Mrs Bláža asked me if I can go over and help her this afternoon.'

Babi raised one eyebrow. She put her open magazine down on the table and studied Luděk's face.

'Help with what?' she said.

Luděk moved his eyes away from hers. He stared at the upside-down magazine print. Blah blah blah blah – that's what the words may as well have said.

'I think she needs to get some stuff down from the cupboards. Cans and things. She can't reach anything.' God, he should have just said she wanted him to pick up some shopping. Something simple.

Babi nodded. 'Be back for lunch,' she said, and she looked down at her magazine again. Then she said, 'You should help her more. She is old and on her own.'

'Yes, Babi,' Luděk said, and he stepped towards the door before he got a lecture about helping the elderly.

'Wait!' Babi said, and she got up off her chair and moved to the cupboard. She got the cake tin down from the top shelf. Inside was a whole bábovka, the one she had made early this morning, and the sight of it made his mouth water. The smell of it, the chocolate and vanilla swirls. Babi cut it in half, and then cut one half in half again. She wrapped a piece up in a clean white tea towel. A whole quarter.

'Take this to Mrs Bláža,' she said. 'And don't you eat any, even if she offers it to you. Don't you dare!'

Luděk nodded. He opened his eyes wide to show that he knew she would find out if he had any. He took the cake in his hands.

What a price to pay.

It was always dark in the stairwell, always gloomy – scary in winter when the wind was howling. Jakub, on the first floor, was practising violin again and the shrill squeals rose up. He was not getting any better. He had no feel for the thing. He just liked playing football, and he was damn fine at that – fast and confident, his feet light and sure. But his father made him play the violin – *Practise, practise, always you must practise!* Bloody Dvořák! Luděk never got to play football with Jakub anymore because Jakub always had to practise. Poor old Jakub.

Out on the street, Luděk looked at the bottom-floor flat across the road. One of the old windows was open, and Old Lady Bláža was there. Just. Luděk could only see the top of her head. She had shrunk so much she could hardly see through her own windows. Luděk didn't know how tall she had been before he knew her, but now she was so bent over it was like the world had crushed her down and squashed her. Soon she would be gone altogether. She must be two hundred years old and her teeth were all gone at the front. She wouldn't even be able to eat the bloody cake. What a waste.

Luděk never spoke to Old Lady Bláža. He tried not to even look at her. He always ran past her as fast as possible, because one time she saw him in the street and called out to him, and then he had to help her with her shopping. He had to get it all to her door. It took forever. She walked so slowly. Why didn't she have a trolley like all the other old ladies?

He had carried the two heavy shopping bags and she had walked behind him – wheezing, panting, coughing. When they got to the flat, Luděk put the bags down just inside her front door, and Old Lady Bláža had reached out and tried to touch his face. Luděk had pulled away, slipped past her and bolted.

Don't touch me with that old crone's hand of death!

Today, he was actually going to have to go into her flat. He was actually going to have to talk to her and maybe even sit down. Maybe even have a cup of her old lady tea. She was the oldest person he knew. She had lived in that flat forever, since the bloody war, and if anyone knew where Atlas was, surely it would be Old Lady Bláža.

Luděk knocked on the door and it fell open.

'Mrs Bláža!' he called. 'Mrs Bláža!' louder this time. A white cat padded up the dark hall and hissed loudly at him. Luděk could not care less about cats. What use were cats? They just wanted things, and once they got them, they ignored you. Cats thought people were a big joke.

Luděk stepped forward, over the threshold now. He stood in the hall, one hand on the open door.

'Mrs Bláža!' he called again, almost yelling the words now. 'Hello!'

Nothing. But he'd seen her by the window, her white hair and the top of her head.

Luděk took a few brave steps down the hall.

There was that smell – the smell of old people, like a dusty museum, a place of no movement. A couch and three armchairs and a coffee table and a footstool and a sideboard and two bookshelves. Old Lady Bláža was still in front of the open window. Standing all bent over the way she did. Her eyes were closed. A patch of sunlight on her face.

'Can you help me, Luděk?' she said, clear as day. Her eyes suddenly open.

How the hell did she know it was him? It could have been anyone yelling from her front door. It could have been anyone standing here. The police, a murderer – anyone.

Old Lady Bláža pointed to the pot plants on the windowsill, and then to a metal watering can that was on the floor. Luděk held up the cake parcel, then put it down on the coffee table.

'This is from Babi,' he said, but she didn't seem to notice. Her eyes looked closed again.

The rusted watering can had water in it but maybe Old Lady Bláža couldn't lift it. How did she even fill it with water to start with? Luděk had no idea how she managed to do anything. He gave her plants a good soaking and he kept going until their little trays were full of water, too. How the hell had the plants survived this long? He knew one of the plants was a geranium, because of the shape of the leaves, and its flowers were bright pink, almost fluorescent. They looked so good there against the white cracked walls of her apartment building. A burst of colour – intense with life.

'Where's Pepík?' Old Lady Bláža said.

Luděk didn't know what the hell she was talking about. Who was Pepík? Her dead husband?

The white cat ran into the room and jumped up on the coffee table. It sat there and stared at Old Lady Bláža.

'Ah,' she said. 'My Pepík!'

The cat started sniffing around the cake and Luděk rushed over and picked it up. The cat sniffed the air.

'This is from Babi,' he said again. 'For you. It's bábovka.' Old Lady Bláža stared at him.

'Marble cake,' he said, and he waved the cake around.

Old Lady Bláža moved past him, one slow step at a time. She waved for him to follow.

The kitchen was very small, but it was clean and there was a white tablecloth on the table just like the one Babi had. Old Lady Bláža lit the gas ring underneath a chipped enamel kettle. When she blew the match out, she snapped it in half and dropped it into an ashtray. The ashtray was full of match halves – one half black, the other half clean and unburnt.

Luděk put the cake on the table. It would go dry, the bábovka, if it wasn't put in a tin soon. Even when it was in a tin, the edges went dry.

'Do you have a tin?' Luděk said.

Old Lady Bláža stared at him.

'A tin for the cake?' Luděk unwrapped the tea towel and showed her.

'Sweet bread,' she said.

Luděk nodded. That's what all the old-timers called cake. Sweet bread. And they only had it for Christmas, or on special occasions. Maybe it was something to do with those saints. The ones no one was meant to believe in anymore.

Old Lady Bláža pointed to a tall cupboard and Luděk opened it. It was crammed with jars and jugs and teapots and bowls, but he found a tin near the back. An old biscuit tin. He opened it and put the cake inside.

'I'll leave this here. It's for you,' he said loudly. And he put the tin down on the table.

He tucked the corner of the white tea towel into his back pocket so he wouldn't forget it.

The kettle started to boil. It had no whistle. Luděk was pretty sure that a whistle would have been useless anyway because it was clear now that Old Lady Bláža couldn't hear much at all. How was he going to ask her about Atlas if she was deaf? This was such a stupid plan.

Old Lady Bláža piled loose tea into the aluminium teapot. Luděk didn't want any tea, but he was stuck now.

Maybe she would offer him some of the cake with the tea? He would have to say no though. Babi *would* find out.

Somehow Old Lady Bláža managed to pour the tea into two cups. She got down a tray, and Luděk thought that there might be biscuits at least, but she just put the two cups on the tray. She waved her hand to Luděk and he picked the tray up. Old Lady Bláža walked slowly back to the lounge and sat down in her chair.

Luděk was very careful not to spill any of the tea. He put the tray down on the coffee table. There were long dark tea leaves resting on the bottom of each cup. He better remember not to drink right to the end. He hated that bitter taste of tea leaves in your mouth. It ruined the whole thing. Why couldn't people use strainers? They did exist. But old people liked the leaves. Old people liked the old ways.

He had to sit there for ages before she drank any of her tea. He sipped his and it was fine. It was good, actually, and the cup was clean. Luděk looked around the room. On the sideboard were framed photographs of people, babies, children, a bride and groom. Everything was dusty.

'Nice,' Old Lady Bláža said, and Luděk didn't know if she meant the tea, or the room, or what, and there was a flash of white, and the cat suddenly jumped in through the open window. It padded down onto the carpet with a thud.

'Oh, Pepík!' Old Lady Bláža said.

Luděk coughed. A bit of tea had gone down the wrong way. The cat stared at him. Its eyes were crazy blue.

'My friend,' Old Lady Bláža said and the cat wound itself around and around her legs, and its purr was so loud Luděk could feel it in his bones.

And this bad feeling busted open inside of him then. In his chest. This old lady had nothing and no one but this dumb white cat. And maybe she was deaf or maybe she just couldn't hear much, but how the hell did she live? She couldn't even listen to the radio.

'I'd better go,' Luděk said and he stood up suddenly. He just wanted to get away now. He put his cup down on the tray. The old lady's eyes went wide and she looked like she might try to get up, like she might try to say something.

Luděk shook his head, waved his hands. 'I can let myself out, Mrs Bláža,' he said, almost shouting.

She nodded then. Smiled. All those missing teeth.

Luděk put both cups on the tray, picked it up and started to walk towards the kitchen. And he heard Mrs Bláža say, with a whistle in her voice. 'I see you – running, running,' and she laughed then. 'So fast!'

Luděk put the tray in the kitchen. He rinsed out the cups. Somehow, he didn't mind that she saw him. Somehow, it didn't bother him.

Back in the lounge, he told Mrs Bláža that he would come back again soon, and she just kept on smiling, kept on nodding. She probably had no idea what he was saying, but he knew that he probably meant it, that he would come back and see her. And he wished he had never come at all, because now he would think about her being all alone.

He walked down the hall and opened the front door. He imagined that Mrs Bláža's eyes were already closed, and maybe she was already asleep, the white cat on her lap purring. And maybe she was dreaming of all the people in the photographs. Dreaming of a time when the ground floor flat was filled with voices and people and life.

Sometimes, when he was alone in the flat, Luděk would sit in the hallway under the phone table and pray that the phone would ring.

Ring!

Ring!

Mama, please call.

He hadn't done it for a long time, but today, when Babi went out to the shops, Luděk crawled under the table and sat against the wall.

He knew their number by heart, 295371. Babi had made him repeat it over and over until there was no way he could forget, and she made him carry an emergency coin at all times in case he needed to use a payphone on the street – if he got into trouble, or if he got lost and could not find his way home. He didn't really need the coin anymore, because he knew how to trick payphones without wasting any money. Uncle Bohdan had taught him that. Uncle could be useful sometimes.

The underside of the phone table had two initials burnt black into the wood – OV. Luděk traced his finger over them. Děda. He had made the phone table with a little seat attached a long time ago. There were photos of Děda, two in Babi's bedroom and a large black and white one in the lounge. Děda's eyes looked straight out of that black and white photograph and into the room – dark eyes just like Mama's.

Luděk had not known him, but Děda was still here in the flat.

The armchair in the lounge, the one in the corner by the window, was Děda's chair. No one ever sat in it, not even Uncle Bohdan, not even Uncle Bill. But the armchair stayed there anyway, as if it was waiting for Děda to come home from work, tired and done in, stepping through the front door and calling out *Hello*. Asking Babi what was for dinner. Taking his shoes off and leaving them on the shoe rack, putting on his slippers, then sitting down in his armchair by the window, his feet resting on the cream footstool.

Ring!
Ring!
Mama, please call.

And it suddenly felt like she was really gone. Forever gone, not just away. Maybe she was never coming back.

Luděk shut his eyes. He tried not to think.

Please call.

That last time on the phone, she had sounded so small. She had almost whispered. She said that she was just tired, that they had been working very hard – night after night, with two shows on Saturday. And maybe it was because *they* were always listening when she called from overseas, and maybe it was because she was trying not to cry, but he could feel it there down the line – something she could not say.

'Where are you going next?' Luděk had asked. He did not know any of the places she told him about. London, Las Vegas, Singapore. He could not picture them. He knew he would never see them, never visit them, but he asked her anyway, about the food and the weather and the hotel breakfasts because he wanted her to keep talking. He wanted to hold on to her for as long as he could.

Luděk put his head in his hands.

Please call.

The front door opened and cold air rushed in, and there was Babi with a bag of shopping, looking down at him.

'LUDOSLAV!'

Luděk stood up and dropped his comic on the bed. He knew he was in for it when Babi called him Ludoslav. She must have found out about something he had done. But what? He stepped into the hall. He tried to think.

Yesterday, at school, he had not eaten his lunch because it was absolutely *dis-gus-ting*. He had to sit there and sit there and sit there, and he could not leave the table until he finished everything on his plate. But he could not eat. He refused. And one of the lunch ladies had written down his name.

He poked his head through the kitchen door. Babi was sitting at the table, her eyes dark like the night.

'Well?' she said.

Luděk stepped forward and threw his arms up to the heavens.

'You don't understand!' he said. 'The lunch ladies – they steal all the good food and give us the slop. You have never seen anyone so FAT. They are scoffing while we –'

'LUDOSLAV!' Babi yelled, and Luděk stopped talking. He closed his mouth.

The cake tin was on the table. The lid was open but there was nothing inside. Not one bit of bábovka. Not. One. Crumb.

His eyes went wide. He had been thinking about that cake all day. He looked at Babi. 'It wasn't me,' he said. 'I didn't take it.'

Babi slapped her heavy hand down on the table. 'You act like I don't feed you – like I don't give you everything!'

'It wasn't me!' Luděk said again.

'What have you done this time?' It was Uncle Bohdan. He walked into the kitchen and stood there grinning like an idiot. He was meant to have fixed the leaking tap in the bathroom but it was still dripping. Luděk could hear it from here. It sounded worse than before.

'Well, I can't fix it,' Uncle Bohdan said, and he wiped his hands on a tea towel. 'I will try and get some parts. Tomorrow. Next day.'

Babi's hard stare was on Uncle Bohdan now.

'That dripping is driving me crazy,' she said.

Uncle Bohdan shrugged, he put the tea towel on the bench. 'Ah! Put a bucket under it. I don't know.'

'A bucket? Luděk could put a bucket under it. Anyone could think of that!'

Uncle Bohdan pulled out a chair and sat down at the table. He sighed.

'I'll fix it,' he said. 'Tomorrow. Next day. I'll fix it,' and his eyes were suddenly on the empty cake tin. Luděk watched his face carefully. He was not grinning now.

'Babi?' Luděk said and he dropped his head down. 'I'm sorry.'

Babi was silent.

'So sorry.'

Luděk looked at the floor, at his feet. His slippers were old. They were faded and old and they were too small. But he could not ask for new ones. He would have to wait – wait for Christmas, wait for Mama to come home. He would have to wait. He heard the sound of the cake tin being shut tight.

'Maybe I will stop making cakes for good. Then you will be sorry,' Babi said. She told Luděk to go to his room and stay there.

Luděk turned and walked to the door. This would all be forgotten soon, but the cake was gone. There would be no cake tonight. No cake this week. No cake for ages. Uncle Bohdan was always scoffing.

'Wait,' Babi said. 'What did you say about school? The lunch ladies?'

Luděk turned slowly. A hot jolt ran up his back, settled on his cheeks. Why had he spilled his guts? When would he ever learn to shut the hell up?

Babi stood up, the cake tin in hand.

'I do not want you calling people fat. You can't go around calling people fat. Do you hear me?'

Yes, Luděk nodded.

Uncle Bohdan was smiling again now. Bloody traitor.

'Do you call me fat behind my back?' Babi said, and she stared at him. His face was trying not to grin, trying not to laugh, but it was starting to crack under the strain.

He shook his head, but he couldn't stop looking at Babi's stomach. She was a bit fat, a bit round, but what did it matter? Babičkas should be a bit fat. When you were old you could get fat like a pig.

'Those lunch ladies *are* fat,' Uncle Bohdan said. 'Everyone knows they steal the meat.'

'See!' Luděk said. He was right. Those lunch ladies were young and fat and they were thieves. 'Someone should call the police!'

Babi's mouth turned up at the ends. She turned away towards the wall. Luděk thought she might be laughing.

'Room!' she said, not looking at him, and Luděk went.

He didn't feel like reading his comic now. He sat on his bed, kicked off his old slippers.

At least the food at school was better than the food at kinder. At school he could get the food down most days. Sometimes it was even good. Sometimes it was even fried potato pancakes. And he was used to school lunches now. But that first day at his new kinder had been the worst.

He had not known what it was on his plate and he'd wanted to cry. Brown things – round and flat and going cold. Brown slop. His teacher told him to eat, to try. But it smelt bad, the food. It smelt like dirt.

'What is it?' he asked.

'Lentils,' the teacher said.

He put one small pea in his mouth and swallowed it down. He ate one at a time, slowly. One damn round slimy lentil at a time. Eventually, he got them all down and was told he could leave the table.

A new kinder. A new place. A new home.

He took his plate up to the lunch lady and told her he was finished. He felt a bit proud that his plate was empty.

'Good boy,' she said. 'A hungry boy.' And before he could say anything she scooped another ladle of lentils onto his plate.

He did cry then. And he was sick on the floor trying to eat this second helping. But when Babi came to get him, she was not angry with him. She hugged him tight and she went crazy at the teacher, crazy at all the lunch ladies.

'Never serve my boy lentils again!' she said.

Her boy.

They walked home together to the warm flat on the third floor, the place where he lived now, and Babi held his hand all the way. She made him his favourite dinner, potato dumplings with bits of bacon. He had no idea where she got the bacon from, but Babi seemed to be able to get things.

He ate it all down, every last bit, and Babi watched him eat.

'Lentils,' she said shaking her head. 'Who serves children lentils?'

Luděk went to the toilet and he listened to the bath tap drip. God, couldn't Uncle Bohdan have left some of the cake? Did he have to eat it all? Between him and Old Lady Blaža, Luděk had not had one bit of that cake.

He washed his hands and dried them on the hand towel. He looked at his face in the mirror, at his blue eyes, at the freckle on his nose. There was a knock at the door and Uncle Bohdan's big head poked around.

'Dinner,' he said.

Luděk turned to him and held out his hand.

Uncle Bohdan stepped into the bathroom. He put his hand in his pocket and pulled out a copper coin – a five-pointed star, twenty haléřů. But Luděk shook his head. This whole cake business was worth more than twenty stinking cents.

Uncle Bohdan sighed. 'Better you than me,' he said.

He fumbled around in his pocket again, then placed a coin in the middle of Luděk's palm. The lady planting crops. One koruna.

Luděk closed his hand up fast, made a fist. Then he screwed his face up at Uncle Bohdan. 'You better fix that stinking tap!' he said.

'Yeah, yeah,' Uncle Bohdan said, waving him off. 'Tomorrow. Next day. Soon.'

A way he had never walked before, a lane he did not know. Cobbled and worn, high walls on either side. At the end, an archway, a gateway, a statue sitting up high. And just like that, he had found him. Just like that, when he wasn't even trying. The statue of a Titan holding up the sky.

Atlas.

His face so tired, his face so strained – muscles bulging out of every limb, out of his calves and his arms and all down his back. The sphere on his shoulders, the weight of it clear. The weight of it pushing into him.

Luděk wanted to speak. He wanted to tell Atlas how he had tried so hard to find him. He didn't have any flowers; he didn't have anything. And it suddenly felt as if he should not be there at all, like this lane was private – a secret. It was not his place.

Atlas. Would Mama know the story? She used to tell him stories, but that was a long time ago now.

Before Papa got sick.

Before Papa died. The tall man he did not really know.

Luděk remembered the stories about The Magician, about trousers that came to life on the washing line, about talking fish, about a flying bicycle. And that's where Mama was now – in the world of stories. Far away, travelling with The Magician, dancing in his theatre.

Fluorescent light – bright against the dark.

Pink and yellow and blue.

A giant spider.

An electric pig.

A week of dreams.

A place of nightmares.

A world where The Magician could bring objects to life.

His mama, graceful and slim in her black velvet suit, hidden from him, but there all the same.

His mama moving light in the dark.

He'd sit and watch the rehearsals, hour after hour. And he loved the lights, the costumes, the music. He loved the whole strange world.

But he didn't like to think about the theatre anymore. He didn't want to think about The Magician.

Luděk looked up at the statue one last time before he turned and walked away. He'd done it. He'd finally found Atlas.

This city was his.

Luděk passed the farmers' stalls full of cabbage.

Goddamn cabbage.

He wished that Czechoslovakia would run out of cabbage. That would NEVER happen unless there was some kind of nuclear war. There was always cabbage. No one ever ran out of cabbage. It was so stupid – you couldn't get bread, but you could always get cabbage. Cabbage soup. Fried cabbage. Pickled cabbage. Cabbage stuffed with more cabbage.

He hoped they would be having schnitzel for lunch. He hoped they would be having meatloaf. He hoped they would be having roast pork. His mouth filled with saliva, but he knew they would not be having any of those things. It could be potato cakes. That was possible. Fried potato cakes. *Please let it be potato cakes. Please let it be something fried.* It would probably be something steamed. Dumplings with cabbage. And if there was cabbage, which there most definitely would be, he would just have to eat it up quick and not chew, so the taste of cabbage would not ruin the taste of the dumplings and the taste of the sauce, so the smell of cabbage would not get up his nose and stay there all afternoon.

Luděk was hungry now, despite the thought of cabbage.

He turned onto his narrow street, the old apartment buildings high on either side. One white, one brown, one light blue, one a faded yellow – the paint cracked and peeling and coming off completely in parts.

In a darkened doorway, a man grabbed a woman and kissed her. His hands slipped down her back towards her round backside. They squeezed in on the tight white material, pinched her firm cheeks hard. They grabbed as much as they could hold. But she did not seem to mind. She just kept on kissing the man.

Luděk felt his cheeks flush. All these people smooching in the shadows – down alleyways and in the back of cars. All this going on and not one thing could stop it. It was this invisible force that was too strong for the world to beat.

A car horn blew. It was Uncle Bohdan. He pulled past slowly, waved out of the window. Luděk waved back. He must have just dropped off some supplies to Babi. Maybe there might be something good for Sunday lunch after all. And Uncle Bohdan would not be there to hog it.

Luděk flew up the stairs, two at a time, to the third floor flat. The door was unlocked and he pushed it open, yelled out, 'Hi! Hi! Hi!' like always. He could smell cooking, lunch, but it was not the smell of frying. Luděk hung his jacket on the coat rack, took off his shoes.

Babi was sitting at the kitchen table, smoking. She did not say hi. Luděk stared at her, at her face, her mouth turned right down against her chin bone.

'Your maminka called,' she said.

Luděk looked up at the wall, at the clock. It was 12.40 pm.

'When?' he asked, and Babi stubbed out her cigarette in the full glass ashtray. She shrugged. She would not meet his eyes. 'An hour, maybe,' she said. Maybe her and Mama had had a fight.

Luděk slumped down on a chair. He was just wearing socks. He had forgotten to put his slippers on, and suddenly there was this weight pressing in on him and he could hardly breathe. He leaned forward, rested his head on the table. How could he have missed the call? While he was out finding a statue. While he was out running around the streets. While he was out looking at a woman's big, firm bottom. How could he have missed Mama's call?

A hand on his head. Babi there next to his chair. She stroked his hair.

'What did she say?' Luděk almost whispered.

'She's in Melbourne. She was at Máňa's place.'

Aunty Máňa who was just here, who gave him his warm jacket, and the too-big denim jeans. Here, just a month ago, now all the way across the world.

Aunty Máňa was free. She could come and go, not like Babi. Not like him. They were stuck here while everyone else in the whole world could move around anywhere they wanted to.

'She says she misses you,' Babi said, 'She loves you.'

Babi's hand was on his shoulder now. It was warm and solid and he felt her take it all like always – take the weight, the bad feelings. They lifted off him and sunk down into her large body. They became solid in her flesh.

'Okay,' Babi said after a while. 'Go and wash up.'

Luděk paused in the doorway. He looked at her – his babi. All those years of carrying so much. All the years of being stuck and having to keep everything going. And he knew that Babi held it all so that he did not have to. Babi held it all so that he could stay free.

He was not like Atlas – but she was.

Eva

21 AUGUST 1968

It is happening again, and now she is on the street trying to walk fast with her shopping in two cloth bags, and the street is clear of cars, clear of trams, and the tanks roll on and on in a thick rumbling line, cracking the old streets – squealing and shrieking in slow motion.

She puts her hand to her forehead, closes her eyes. She tries not to faint, and one of the shopping bags falls from her hand. A jar of gherkins rolls out along the street towards the moving tanks. It does not break.

The Soviet flags fly. The huge guns point ahead.

'You should get home.' A voice behind her – soft. A man, bright eyes burning.

He bends down, picks up her shopping. He puts the gherkin jar back in the bag.

'Those bastards!' he says. He is young, maybe a student. She is old. She cannot do this again. She cannot fight anymore.

'You should get home,' he says again. She takes the bag. She nods.

Home.

She starts to walk along the street in the opposite direction to the tanks. It is still early, and the streets are filling with people on their way to work. It seems like nobody knows what to think, or how to be – but people are pale. People are serious.

She keeps on walking, away from the tanks and the smell of thick diesel smoke.

No one is coming. Just like before. No one is coming to save them.

The Curtain will become solid, made of steel and concrete, and it will not bend, it will not open. They are all stuck inside – forgotten. They must all go to sleep.

She keeps on walking.

She must get home.

Melbourne
1980

Huge yellow wheels of cheese sit behind the glass.

The man behind the counter gives me a slice. It is the kind that has round holes in it like the cheese in cartoons. It is the cheese I like best because it doesn't really smell like cheese.

'Say *thank you*,' my grandma says, and I do. The man winks at me. People know us at the market because we come almost every day.

At the bread counter, my grandma buys three Kaiser rolls, and the woman hands them to her in a paper bag. My grandma pays with coins from her purse, but instead of moving away, she stands there moving coins around with her finger. There is a man right behind us, and he keeps moving his feet, shuffling. He keeps sighing. I don't want to turn around and look at him. I look ahead.

'Do you have any rye bread with caraway left?' My grandma asks and the woman behind the counter turns. She checks the rows of loaves.

'None left,' she says.

'I'll take the normal rye,' my grandma says, and the woman grabs a loaf.

'Oh, not the dark one, the light rye please,' my grandma says, her eyes wide and the woman puts the dark rye back on the shelf. She picks out a loaf of light rye.

The man behind us is tapping his foot now, banging it hard on the ground. He sighs again. 'Hurry up, stupid wog,' he says suddenly.

I stand very still.

My grandma smiles at the woman behind the counter. She hands over the money for the rye, the coins, and she puts the wrapped loaf in her fabric shopping bag.

'Thank you,' she says in her best accent. She takes my hand, and we walk away from the bread counter, and away from the man. I turn and see his blue jeans and his black shoes – the ones that were tapping against the concrete.

I look up at my grandma, and she looks completely normal – her face still like stone. But then a tear, just a small one, spills down her soft, powdered cheek and she does not wipe it away.

———⚡———

My grandma never spoke to me about what happened. We never talked about it, and my grandma did not tell my grandpa about the man at the market when we got home.

I did not know what the word *wog* meant, but I knew that it felt like a giant spotlight suddenly shone on my grandma to make sure that everybody knew she did not belong. To make sure she felt ashamed of her accent, ashamed of her face, ashamed of the way she loved the taste of caraway seeds in her light rye bread.

'Who watches the tennis?' my grandpa asks.

'The bourgeois,' I answer.

My grandpa gets up out of his armchair and he moves towards the TV at pace, like he is going to change the channel, or even turn the TV off altogether. My grandma throws a couch pillow at his head, but he catches it with ease. He winks at me, hands me the pillow.

'Right, I'm going to bed,' he says. His afternoon nap before he has to become a night watchman.

Grandma pats the space on the couch next to her. That means, *Come and sit with me.* I do. I give her the pillow and she puts it behind her head and leans back.

The match has started. There's that *whack* of tennis balls being smashed hard against the tight strings of rackets. And there is a lot of grunting. But there is *no* clapping. People can only clap quickly when a point or game or match is won. I can only talk quickly when a point or game or match is won.

'Fifteen–love.'

———⚡———

My grandma loved the tennis. If a Czech player was playing she loved it even more. If a Czech player was playing, my grandpa even watched for a few minutes. If Ivan Lendl was playing, then my grandpa might even watch the whole match with us.

I didn't really like the tennis, but I think it was probably my grandma's favourite thing. It was only on the TV in summer. I was glad it wasn't on all year round because by the end of the summer I had really had enough of it. Tennis meant less time in the lounge listening to music and playing cards. It meant less trips out in the afternoon. Tennis meant sitting for hours in the hot lounge room listening to a man say, 'Fifteen–love.'

I'd watch my grandma's bare feet resting on her footstool. They would flinch every so often with the action on the screen, with the flying tennis balls.

My grandma's legs resting.

Good to get off her feet.

Good to rest.

All that weight.

My grandma's soles were thick, solid like concrete slabs. She used a pumice stone and it lived on the corner of the green bath top. It worked very hard, that stone. All the weight it tried to scrub away but never could. All the weight her feet carried, heavy and solid.

But she could be light on her feet sometimes, my grandma. Light somehow when you least expected it. Sometimes she even seemed weightless – like when she'd come into the lounge in the morning with her girdle half on and say, 'Pull me up!'

I'd stand on the couch, balancing as best I could, and I'd grab onto the tight tan material. I'd try to get my fingers right in under the thick cross-hatched stitching, and *I would pull!*

I'd pull up against my grandma's ample flesh using all my strength. I'd pull against the bulging, rolling waves. I'd feel her soft brown skin against my fingers and *I would pull!*

And it felt like I was pulling her body right up into the air. I'd imagine her feet off the ground, her legs dangling free. She seemed to hover there for a time, like she was up in space.

I know it is impossible. She was too big, too heavy, and I was only small.

Still, I have the feeling of it in my hands – lifting her up into the air. My grandma.

When that underwear-armour covered everything except her arms and legs, my grandma would pat the sides of her girdle, finally ready for the day. I'd watch her walk to her bedroom, her feet moving quickly. No stomping, no sound – as if her body was somewhere far away and the person I could see was just a projection. A silent film.

She'd get dressed. Put on her tights and one of her bright nylon dresses. She'd fix her long hair in a high beehive, spray it tight with hairspray. She'd do her face, finish it off with powder that smelt like fresh rose-petals. Then it would be time for the market. We would leave the flat, walk down the stairs together, and my grandma would hold my hand all the way to the market and all the way home. We would eat lunch in the kitchen with my grandpa, clean up – and my grandma would make some coffee so it would be ready when the tennis started on the TV.

Then the man would say over and over, 'Fifteen–love, thirty–love, forty–love, game, set, match.'

Apricots. A pile of them on the green kitchen table – already halved and pitted, the centres oozing all sweet and sticky.

My grandma kneads the dough. I kneel on my seat, rest down on my elbows and watch my grandma's big, strong hands work. She cuts the dough into small, even squares. I listen for the door, listen to the clock tick. My grandpa is late.

My grandma spreads flour on the table and picks up her first square. She pinches it into a circle with her thumbs and forefingers and when it is thin enough, she wraps the dough around an apricot half, seals up the ends tight.

Apricot dumplings.

My grandma works fast, her hands in constant movement until there are no more apricot halves on the table. She sorts the finished dumplings into groups of six and puts each group in a small plastic bag. She knots the bags tightly. Like always, the fresh dumplings are going into the freezer. Like always, there are six dumplings in each bag. Two for me. Two for my grandpa. Two for my grandma. Everything fair. Everything even. For special occasions.

My grandma wipes down the table, cuts through the dusty flour with a wet sponge, and I finally hear the front door. The key and that heavy click when the door closes, then my grandpa's slow steady steps down the hall. My grandma and I watch the door. My grandpa walks into the small kitchen quietly, and he looks tired. He looks crumpled.

'The factory has let me go,' he says.

Just like that.

He tells us that he will get six weeks' pay and that he will no longer be night watchman.

'Too old,' he says.

My grandpa has lost his job. He is sixty-one years old.

He leans against the sink, looks at nothing. 'I will look for another job,' he says.

The clock ticks. The room is still. Even my grandma's busy hands no longer move.

'Go and have a shower,' my grandma says, and my grandpa leaves the kitchen as quietly as he came in.

———⚡———

After his hot shower in the mornings, my grandpa always ate a small breakfast in the kitchen before he went to bed.

He never talked while he ate his breakfast, even when I sat with him. He never talked, he just ate. Maybe he was happy to have the company, and maybe he was annoyed to have the company, but I knew not to ask him any questions then because he was already half asleep, and the talking, the words, and all the thinking would wake him up – wake his brain. Then he would *wrestle with his blankets*. He would toss and turn in his little bed until he could no longer stand it, the strain of trying to sleep, and he would get up again and sit in his chair and smoke his pipe.

Those days were the bad days. Too much sleep pushing down on him but unable to settle. He would be a ghost on those days, moving through that third storey flat not really there. I would sit and be quiet, and I'd play patience – a game my grandpa taught me especially for those days – and I would count out the cards in my head, and not out loud like normal.

I wished that my grandpa could sleep, but I knew that sometimes he could not. And I thought that maybe it was a good thing he wouldn't have to be a night watchman anymore because now he could sleep at night while we were sleeping. He no longer had to sleep alone. We could all be together in sleep, and that would be good.

The day my grandpa became redundant, my grandma left two bags of apricot dumplings out of the freezer and set them aside. They were my grandpa's favourite – boiled apricot dumplings with melted butter and sugar and cottage cheese on top.

Food for special occasions – for emergencies. And my grandma let my grandpa eat six. A whole bowl full of steamed apricot dumplings – soft and sweet and filling.

My grandpa found a part-time job delivering the *Truth* newspaper. The pay was no good, but it was better than nothing, and my grandpa hated not working. He no longer sorted through his coins in the afternoons, and the gherkin jar was put away in a cupboard.

The paper only came out once a week, so for the rest of the time my grandpa tinkered with things in his workshop, which was in the small garage. That way he didn't get under my grandma's feet. He ate more, and he slept more. He would go out for long walks by himself and I knew not to ask if I could go with him. The flat had become too small.

My grandpa looked forward to Fridays when it was time to go to work. Sometimes I would go with him to deliver the *Truth* in the Ford Telstar.

My grandpa would always get to the printers early on Friday afternoons, and we would wait in the car until it was time to load up the *Truth* in the boot and back seat and anywhere they could fit. My grandpa would ask me questions about politics while we waited. Who is the Prime Minister of Great Britain? *Margaret Thatcher.* Who is the Father of Communism? *Karl Marx.* When was the eight-hour day won for the workers? *1856.* What is the Munich Agreement?

'What is the Munich Agreement?'

There is silence and I don't know the answer.

'No one cared about us,' my grandpa says, and he turns to me. 'My home shrunk by one third – can you imagine?'

I shake my head.

My grandpa stares out the window then, and his cheeks are going red, and his breath is fast.

'People wonder how Hitler took my country without one shot being fired. Well – it was handed to him on a silver plate!'

I have never heard my grandpa talk like this, all fast and jumbled, the words spitting out, his accent sharp and not hidden. Not soft.

I look at the glove compartment. I know what is inside – a copy of the Melways 1979, and a can of WD40. There are also two screwdrivers, a Phillips head screwdriver with a green handle, and a plain screwdriver with a yellow handle. My grandpa always says that you never know when you might need a screwdriver, or some WD40. But my grandpa never uses the Melways. He knows his way around the streets of Melbourne. He is very good with directions.

'Platter,' my grandpa says. 'I mean silver platter not plate.'

He is calmer again, his cheeks not so flushed. We sit there waiting. He hands me a peppermint. My grandpa always has a roll of peppermints in his pocket. Extra strong. They burn my mouth, make my eyes water – but I can never resist. I always take one.

'One shot *was* fired,' my grandpa says, 'from your great-grandfather, if you don't mind.' And he looks at me now, his eyes alive.

'He did not hit one single thing. He fired out the window and the bullet went into the sky.'

Finally, the papers are being put out on the loading dock in giant piles.

'Still, he paid the price,' my grandpa says. 'My father.'

I want to ask my grandpa what his father's name is – was – but I don't ask. And my grandpa gets out of the Ford Telstar and begins to fill the boot with the *Truth*.

Each newsagent had their own pile of *Truth*s that needed to be delivered and we would do many trips back to the printers on each run. Sometimes I would help my grandpa actually deliver the papers when he couldn't find a park and had to double-park. And he would tell me to take them to the newsagent door, put them down, and then yell out, 'TRUTH!', as loudly as I could manage.

I liked that bit, yelling out 'Truth!'. It made me laugh because when I yelled it, it came out as 'TROOOF'. My grandpa would give me twenty cents for the day, for helping. He would always say, 'Don't tell your grandma', and I never did.

Máňa

28 SEPTEMBER 1938

My heart is racing, my face burns. From the podium, the stadium looks so big and the crowd is cheering and I feel dizzy.

A strong mind in a sound body, the crowd chants together, the stadium alive with pride. The world has let us down, thrown us away, but we stand tall. Three hundred and fifty thousand of us, our national anthem sung over and over. We are here!

There is a blazer just for me, navy with the emblem of the falcon, pressed and brand new. It is the nicest thing I have ever owned. There is a gold pin on the lapel, a gold pin with my name engraved on it. Máňa Králová.

I am head girl.

I know Eva is angry. She thinks she is as good as me. She thinks she should be head girl. But I know I try harder, work harder. I practise harder. And this is all I have ever wanted. Fit and strong. I will train and become a teacher. I will lead the next generation.

The right for every child to fulfil their potential. The words ring out in my head and I believe in them. My potential.

The park is full, colourful and alive, and it feels like the music from the stadium is still playing, and that we are all still dancing. The performers and the crowd mix together like one giant animal moving towards the city in the gentle darkness. Evening.

Eva pulls at my arm.

'I'm cold,' she says, and she keeps on saying it, she keeps pulling at me until I give her the blazer. Sulking – still sulking, even with all the joy around us. She puts the blazer on, and it looks good on her. She is me. We are the same. It fits well, and I can't wait to show Papa.

We cross the bridge and the crowd fills it completely from side to side and end to end. We have brought our city to a standstill. We have brought our city to life. On the other side, people hang out of apartment windows and wave our Czech flag. People cheer, *We won't be taken!*

The crowd begins to thin, veins of people walking in all directions. The sun has dropped completely now and even though there are lots of people still around, the streets feel more gloomy, more normal. The everyday streets. We cross the square, turn off towards home, and I feel tired suddenly, adrenaline gone. I tell Eva to give me back my blazer. I want Papa to see me wearing it when we come through the door, but she won't. She starts to run and she is far ahead before I catch up. She flies down the street and around the corner and I trip on a cobble and fall. But I'm not hurt. I get up, I sprint as fast as I can until I can almost touch Eva's back, touch my blazer with my fingertips. Eva is laughing, squealing, not sulking anymore.

'Give it back,' I scream, and suddenly there is a man right in front of us, a man wearing a hat, and Eva runs into him with full force. She flies backwards, hits the pavement hard right by my feet. The man must have come out of a doorway. He just came out of nowhere. His hat is in the gutter.

'I'm sorry,' Eva says, looking up at the man, looking right into his face. His head is balding and I pick up his grey hat. It's wet with grime from the deep gutter. He moves forward and snatches it from my hands. His cheeks are sweaty, his eyes pinched.

'Why can't you watch where you are going,' he says. His words strained, his accent strange. 'Running like dogs!'

Eva gets to her feet. The blazer is covered in dirt all down the back. It is torn near the bottom. It is ruined.

'I'm sorry,' Eva says again, and the man comes towards her. He stands very close. His hand comes down, touches the blazer emblem, touches the gold pin on the lapel. My gold pin.

'Máňa Králová,' he says. And he grabs both of Eva's arms. He pulls her in, their faces almost touching.

'I see you're proud of your little country, of your little dancing.'

Eva nods. Her face pale.

The man says something, his hands still tight on Eva's arms. I want to pull her away, I want to help, but I'm frozen. And I understand the words.

'You socialist pig.'

German.

The man rips the gold pin off the blazer, clutches it in his fist. Then he spits right in Eva's face.

I grab her arm and tug her away, and we start to run, holding onto each other. When I turn back, the man is gone. He is nowhere and there is no one. No one in the windows, no one in the street. No flags, no colour. No life.

Eva begins to sob.

'I should never have let you go,' Papa says, and he sits with his head in his hands.

I stare at him, at his dark hair going grey.

'Papa?' I say. 'Papa?'

He stays seated. He looks at the floor.

'They are coming,' he says, quietly – almost a whisper. 'Coming.'

'We will fight them, Papa,' Eva says. 'We will fight them and win.'

Papa shakes his head. He looks up now, looks right into my eyes.

'Tomorrow they take one third of our country. Soon that won't be enough for them. We must get you out.'

'But it was my fault. It was me!' Eva cries out.

Papa looks at her, and then back at me. He takes both of my hands in his – big and rough. He is shaking.

'It will be okay,' he says, and his eyes go to the floor once more. He breathes in deeply, breathes out. 'Maybe this war will be short, and then you can come back to us.'

He does not believe his words, I know that. I start to cry then, and I fall into my papa's arms. I cry and Eva cries and Papa cries, and he holds us tight. He won't let go.

We sleep as one in the same bed. We cling to each other. We say each other's names over and over.

Máňa, Madlenka, Maruška, Mařenka, Majka, Márinka.

Eva, Evka, Evička, Evinka, Evelína, Lina.

I'm sorry. Don't go.

I'm scared. I don't want to go.

Eva wants me to take the ocarina – Mama's bluebird. Papa was right to give it to her, she can play so well. Eva makes that bird sing happy songs. I am no good at it. I can't play. I wanted it so badly once, this clay bird, and I hold it softly in my hands as if it is alive, as if its heart beats fast and it might fly away.

'You can give it to me when I come home,' I say.

Eva nods but her eyes won't find mine.

Papa paid for stolen papers – somehow.

Only enough money for one.

'Don't ever sell your earrings, Máňa,' he says. 'Hold on to them. Keep hold of them.'

And I know that I will never see my papa again. I know this is goodbye.

A passage to London.

A little brown suitcase.

A skirt.

A blouse.

A cardigan.

My old winter coat.

My brown shoes.

Papa's English dictionary – his name written on the inside cover.

I am alone now. Completely. I must become Marie. No soft names, no nicknames. Not Máňa, just Marie.

I am alone.

Prague
1980

Uncle Bohdan struggled to get the colour TV up the three flights of stairs. He had to put it down several times to rest, and when he finally got it inside the flat, sweat was pouring out of him, down his neck and springing from his forehead. Uncle Bohdan was not a small man.

He stood with his hands on his hips, breathing hard. Babi got him a towel.

The TV was Russian, a Rubin – like the black and white one Babi had watched forever. But this new one was bulky and there were lots of different dials, lots of sliding controls. Babi sat in her chair and stared at the large blank screen while Uncle Bohdan got down on all fours on the carpet and strained to plug in the cord.

'Okay,' he said when he finally hit the socket.

Luděk flicked the switch and stared as the screen opened its eyes. It was colour – full, bright colour, but it was strange. It was all wrong. People's faces were crazy and the sky was a kind of orange. Every few seconds the whole screen flashed fluorescent green. It pulsed and flickered like a beating heart, like it was alive.

'Get the instructions,' Uncle Bohdan said and waved his hand towards the cardboard box.

Luděk fished around in the box and handed the manual to Uncle Bohdan. Uncle Bohdan stared at it blankly. It was in Russian.

Babi was still watching the screen and she kept saying, 'Oh,' every now and then as things that were not meant to be yellow turned bright yellow. That hospital serial she liked was on, the one that was boring as hell with the *handsome* doctor that all the ladies loved.

Uncle Bohdan started sliding the vertical colour controls: up – halfway – down. Up – halfway – down. At one point the screen looked almost normal – the grass was green, the sky was blue, but it did not last. Uncle Bohdan moved another control and the picture faded down to a kind of black and white. Black and white with highlights of bright colour. Black and white with fluorescent edges.

Uncle Bohdan stood back from the TV. He shook his head. 'Another great product from our Soviet comrades,' he said, and he walked away from the TV and out of the lounge.

But Babi seemed pleased, her eyes still fixed on the screen, on the unfolding drama. An ambulance sped along the road to the scene of a car crash, the handsome doctor ready for action.

The TV was much bigger than their old TV and the sound was clear – crisp. That was something at least. It *was* an upgrade.

'What will we do with the old one?' Luděk asked. The old black and white workhorse. Thirteen years old and still going.

Uncle Bohdan returned to the lounge with a bottle of beer.

He did not want the old TV. He had a better one. And he did not want the hassle of trying to off-load it.

'Maybe we can give it to Mrs Bláža?' Luděk said.

Babi squinted her eyes. She turned away from the TV and looked right inside of him. The moment went on and on and Luděk tried not to blink.

'She doesn't have a TV,' Luděk said. 'Or even a radio.'

Babi's eyes softened – relaxed.

'You're a good boy,' she said, and she slapped Uncle Bohdan on the legs.

'Help Luděk take the TV,' she said.

Uncle Bohdan's forehead was still sweating. He took a massive gulp of beer. Then another. Babi slapped his legs again.

'Okay! Okay!' he said and he put his beer down on the coffee table.

The black and white TV was much lighter than the colour set, but the loose cord nearly made Uncle Bohdan trip down the stairs.

'Luděk!' he shouted, trying to see over the television resting on his belly.

Luděk grabbed the cord and walked behind his uncle – one slow step at a time.

Mrs Bláža didn't seem to know what was happening when they walked into her flat carrying the TV, but when Luděk switched it on, her face opened up. She sat down in her chair, rested one hand on her cheek.

'There are two channels,' Luděk said, and he turned the knob, *click*, to channel 2. He looked at her, nodded. The hospital show was still on. He turned the knob backwards, *click*, to channel 1.

'This one is the best one,' he said.

She couldn't hear, he knew that. She had no idea what he was saying. Her eyes stared at the images that were on the screen. Farmland, tractors, co-operatives. The country – a place he had never been. A place where everyone worked hard and smiled under a shining sun.

Uncle Bohdan cleared his throat and Luděk looked over. He was standing in the middle of the lounge with his arms folded across his chest. He wanted to go, get back to his beer.

'I'll stay,' Luděk said, and Uncle Bohdan turned and walked right out of the room without saying a single word.

Luděk turned the TV slightly so Mrs Bláža could see it from her armchair. Uncle Bohdan had just plonked it down on a sideboard because there was no TV stand in the room. Luděk hoped it was okay there, and that Mrs Bláža would not try to lift it. If she tried to move it, she might kill herself.

Mrs Bláža's eyes were still on the screen. Maybe she wouldn't even watch it much, but it was nice that she could if she wanted to, just like everyone else.

Luděk checked to see if the plants needed watering, but they all looked good, the soil damp. He looked around the room for the cat, but Pepík was nowhere to be seen.

An old movie came on – the Sunday afternoon movie, the ones that Babi liked to watch. Luděk often watched them with her, to keep her company. He thought Mrs Bláža would like this kind of movie, one from the old days.

'I'd better go,' Luděk said. But Mrs Bláža's eyes were closed now, her chin resting down against her chest.

Luděk turned off the TV, and he heard the tube inside power down. He patted it. It had been a pretty good TV, even if it was Russian. He would come back tomorrow to check if Mrs Bláža remembered how to turn it on, how to use it. He would come back tomorrow and make sure.

The flat door was open – the TV softly on. Mrs Bláža was in her chair, the cat curled up on her lap, and Luděk stood close. He said her name, reached out and touched her green cardigan with his fingertips.

Luděk stayed standing by the chair, and the cat looked up at him. Luděk held its gaze, and the moment went on for a long time.

He walked over to the TV and switched it off. It was warm and the screen closed to black – the giant eyelid shutting for the last time.

Silence.

The cat jumped down from Mrs Bláža's lap onto the old carpet and walked towards Luděk's feet. It padded around his legs, rubbing its body against Luděk's skin. It was purring.

'Come on,' Luděk said, and he picked up the large cat, held it tightly in his arms.

He carried it past all the dusty picture frames that lined the sideboard, all the black and white photographs of people staring into the camera. Weddings and babies and children gathered around the glowing candles on a birthday cake. Where were they now? Why hadn't they been there to help? This city was full of old women left behind. Left to keep everything going – to carry the whole goddamn world by themselves.

He took one more look at Mrs Bláža in her chair – her apron still on – and he walked down the hall. He shut the front door gently behind him, Pepík safe in his arms, still purring.

A big truck came to take things away, to clear Mrs Bláža's ground storey flat. Luděk watched it all from the street, watched the men carrying furniture out, carrying boxes. Babi came down wearing her coat and sat on the stone step. The air did not move and she did not speak. She smoked a cigarette and looked ahead. She smoked another. She was remembering the dead. She was thinking about the people who were no longer here.

How's your husband?

Dead.

Your son-in-law?

Dead.

Your cousin?

Dead.

How's your daughter?

Gone.

Gone, but not dead.

Babi put out her cigarette, squashed it into the stone. She caught Luděk's eye. She was alive. Luděk was alive. The white cat sleeping in their flat was alive. It was enough.

When the truck finally pulled away, full of old things, Mrs Bláža's plants were left behind on the pavement. Luděk asked if he could take them, because the nights were getting cold and they might freeze, but Babi said he could only have one. He chose the geranium – the one with the bright flowers. He worried about what would happen to all the other plants, but by morning they were all gone, safe inside other people's flats.

Mrs Bláža's geranium bloomed pink fluorescent on the kitchen windowsill – so brilliant it lit up the room.

Luděk looked after it.

A postcard on the kitchen table. Lots of bright cars and tall buildings and a blue, blue sky. Greetings from Melbourne.

Luděk held it in his hands. He read the words written in black pen on the back.

My darling boy,
    I am coming home –
And I will never leave you again.
    Maminka xxx

He had collected programs from all of his mother's tours. She would save him one from each city, and they were mostly in English – but sometimes in French or Spanish or Italian. And there was a picture of her in each program – her face, her dark eyes. And there was always an ad for Czechoslovak Airlines on the back of each program, and it would say, 'The Black Theatre of Prague Fly on Czechoslovak Airlines.' Now Czechoslovak Airlines was going to fly his mama home. She would take off in a whole different place, fly up in the sky, and then land down in Prague. She was coming home.

Ludĕk got out of bed and snow was falling.

He did not love snow. It got trampled into hard ice quickly and all the stairs became giant stone slides. Black ice and bloody snow. Whoosh, someone was always going down right in front of him, going down hard on their backsides. Ludĕk couldn't move fast in the snow. He couldn't run. He had to walk carefully like everyone else or end up on his backside, too, with sodden, freezing pants. It was only October and he felt cheated to have the last bit of autumn ripped away. You never knew when winter was going to creep up.

'Ludĕk!'

He got some socks out of the drawer and put them on his bare feet.

Babi was standing in the hall holding on to a ladder, the manhole to the roof space open.

'Can you find the sled?' she said.

Luděk stared at her. He had never seen a sled, never heard of a sled. If there was a sled he would have been using it every winter on the streets and on the hills.

'Up the back – behind the boxes.'

Luděk hated getting in the roof space. It was dark and it was dusty and it smelt bad like old rotting leaves.

He stepped up the rungs of the ladder in his socks and put his head through the manhole. He could only see near the entrance where the light sliced in. Boxes, bags, an old worn suitcase.

'Up the back,' Babi yelled, and she tapped the back of his legs with her hand. He continued moving up the ladder.

The space was small and the roof pitched just above his head. He wished he had put on shoes now. His socks would get wrecked, and he might stand on a nail or a spider or an old dead rat.

'Luděk?'

God, couldn't she give him a minute? Even if he found a sled, what did she want with it, anyway?

Luděk let his eyes get used to the low light. Everything was packed in so tight. He slid a box out of the way and dust whooshed into the air and went up his nose. He blinked his eyes, held a sneeze. What was all this stuff? Some of it must be Mama's things. Mama's records would be up here. He wanted to get one out, put it on Děda's stereo in the lounge and listen.

He slid another box out of the way and touched the slanting roof with his hand until he reached the end of the space. Now he had to get down on his knees to fit. He felt around, felt the floor, felt the wall – there was something right up the back. Something wooden, and rounded. A sled.

'It's here,' he called.

'What?' Babi yelled. Her head appeared at the top of the ladder in the square of light. She was squinting.

'I found it,' Luděk said.

'Can you bring it down?'

Luděk didn't answer. Was she drunk? How would he get it down? He rubbed his eyes. Dust had got in and they had begun to itch.

'Luděk?'

'Okay,' he said.

Babi disappeared back down the ladder.

It was not easy moving the sled. It was heavy and awkward – and it would only fit through the manhole on an angle. If Luděk dropped it, he might kill Babi. It might bust a hole in the floor as well. He told Babi to get out of the way, but she hovered right underneath him, hopping from one foot to the other. Luděk stepped onto the ladder and eased the sled out of the hole.

'Don't drop it!' Babi said.

Luděk couldn't speak. He had the full weight of the sled against his chest now and he stepped quickly down the rungs – down, down, sliding the sled against the ladder. When he stepped onto the floor, the sled slipped down with a thud.

Babi's eyes were wide.

'I won't be able to get it back up there,' Luděk said. 'Uncle Bohdan will have to do it.'

But Babi didn't say anything. She just kept staring at the sled.

It was handmade and ancient, and the wooden slats had been painted once – maybe dark green, or dark blue, but the paint was mostly gone. But the two curved feet still looked good, solid. Babi ran her hand over the seat and pressed down. The slats let out a little squeal.

'Okay,' she said. 'Get your snow gear out.'

Luděk stared at her.

'Go on, before I change my mind and make you go to school.'

Luděk's snow gear was old and tight as hell. God, he'd grown. His pants were too short and his ankles would freeze. Babi got him an extra pair of socks and he pulled them up as far as they would go. He put on the striped beanie Babi had made him. It was okay, except for the big pom-pom on the top. He wished she hadn't put that on. But he had his new coat, the parka from Aunty Máňa, and that was something. It was like a spacesuit, and no one else would have one like it.

Luděk pulled the wooden sled along the streets and it slushed slowly through the thick snow. There was not one car moving. You could sled down any street you wanted, sled anywhere. The whole city had turned into a playground and kids were slipping and screaming and sliding in every direction. He wasn't the only one lucky enough to get out of school that day.

Babi did not seem to worry about slipping over like she normally did when it snowed. She walked fast, she marched on and on, not stopping once and Luděk was puffed keeping up.

God, this sled must be as old as Mama, or even older. It was a bit embarrassing having such an old sled, and being with Babi. Other kids had metal sleds that they carried easily on their backs. Other kids were with their siblings or friends. They were not with their grandmothers.

Finally, they got to the parkland and Luděk could see the hill. Petřín Hill – the best place to sled in the whole city.

Luděk thought they should start from halfway up the hill just to test the sled. He was worried about how he was going to steer it, how he was going to stop. But Babi kept on marching right to the top. He'd tell her that he would do a solo run first, and then he would bring the sled back up. But Babi sat down on the seat and told Luděk to sit in front of her. He shook his head. She might break her back. She might die.

'Luděk!' Babi said.

He sat down.

The seat creaked and moaned, and before he could get his feet wedged in against the frame, Babi kicked them off with her foot. Luděk grabbed the sides of the sled as they started moving. They were not going too fast, not yet – and maybe this would be okay. Maybe it would be fine and the sled would be slow because it was so old. But then they picked up speed, slipped into a well-worn track on the steepest part of the hill, and the weight of the sled was pulling them down faster, pulling them down harder. Luděk could hardly see, and the cold air whipped past his face and made his eyes water. He hoped they weren't heading towards any trees. He hoped people would get out of their way. Then his stomach flipped. He felt the sled lift off the ground – up – up – and for a moment they were flying. For a moment they were soaring through the air.

Luděk lay on his back and looked up at the white sky. Snowflakes fell on his face and melted on his skin. He wriggled to sit up. Babi was lying flat on her back in the snow, the sled on its side.

'Are you okay?' Luděk said.

Babi was making strange sounds like she was choking, and Luděk stood up. He ran over and looked down at her face.

She was laughing.

'I think the sled is broken,' Luděk said. And it was broken. Bits of it had cracked off completely.

Babi's whole body was shaking now. She put her hands on her cheeks. 'Oh, Luděk!' she said. And she laughed even harder. 'We flew. We flew!'

Luděk had never seen her like this, and now he was smiling, too.

They *had* flown.

'Are you okay?' Luděk asked again, and he held out his hands and helped her to sit up. Her short, curled hair was full of snow and tears rolled down her face.

'Thank you,' she said, still giggling.

'Are you upset about the sled?' Luděk said.

Babi shook her head and got to her feet. She wiped snow off her pants, shook snow out of her hair.

'It went out with a bang,' she said.

Babi picked up a few pieces of broken sled, and piled them on the main body.

'My papa made this sled,' she said. 'For me and Máňa.'

Luděk looked at her wide eyes, and it was like he could see a movie there, one that she was watching, too. Two sisters sledding and laughing and running in the snow. Two sisters dressed in woollen hats and woollen coats, wearing the same brown leather boots. Two sisters playing and dreaming and laughing. Before the war. Before everything.

For all the time he had known Babi, she had been old. She was his babi, his grandma. He had never thought of her as young. He had never thought of a life before him.

'Maybe your mother can get you a new sled,' Babi said. 'One of those metal ones.'

Luděk nodded. They started walking.

He wanted to ask if Mama was better now – if Mama was okay, not like before – but he didn't ask. Maybe he was scared of the answer. Maybe he didn't want Mama to come back. He could stay with Babi, stay in the flat. It had been his home for so long. Just him and Babi. He couldn't leave her alone. He wouldn't go.

'I thought your mother should stay in Australia,' Babi said. 'To have a better life.'

Luděk could hear the broken sled struggle to slide and he had to pull it hard. Babi stopped walking, turned to face him.

Luděk looked down at his old rubber boots.

'I wrecked it,' he said, 'for Mama. Didn't I?'

He could hear Babi's breath – hard, alive. She put an arm around him and pulled him in.

'She loves you. She is coming home because she loves you.'

Luděk looked up at her face. He knew she was telling the truth.

'It will all be okay,' Babi said. 'I promise.'

He almost cried then, because he did want Mama to come home. He wanted it more than anything.

'I have lived so long without my sister, without those I love, and I am used to it. But that won't be your life.'

Luděk put his head against her strong frame and hugged her back. And he didn't care who saw him. His babi.

The Magician

1978

My city has become darker – almost blacked out. And we are shut in.

I see it everywhere – the lost, the broken.

This Kingdom of Forgetting.

I must work harder.

I must see differently.

Where there is only black, I will see colour.

Where there is only black, I will see in fluorescent light.

I collect the broken and put them in my suitcase. I take them with me – my actors, my dancers. I make them see in light.

I put the broken in my suitcase and take them with me until they are ready to go home again.

There is still love.

Tábor
1981

Mama used her savings from the theatre to buy a white Fiat 127. She gave the pea-green Wartburg to Uncle Bohdan for good. She bought Babi a trip to Australia to thank her for all she had done.

The Fiat was new and shiny and it had a tape player with good speakers. But now Aleš sat in the passenger seat next to Mama, and there was a baby in the back next to him. But that was okay. That was fine.

His little sister.

They no longer lived in the city, but they still listened to rock and roll, and when the Rolling Stones came on, Mama always sang along. Luděk could wind the window down whenever he wanted because the air was clean and clear and no one minded if their hair got messed up. But sometimes Luděk missed the flat on the third floor, just

him and Babi, no one else. He missed his city, where he
ran and ran the old streets and was invisible.

Down a lane, up the stone stairs – Luděk runs. Short skirts,
mothers in their summer dresses pushing prams. Another
carefree Saturday.

An old man and his wife hold hands. They walk slowly
on the uneven cobbles. You have to watch where you step.
You have to walk like a duck on the old stones. Luděk zips
around the corner, the river up ahead with the glowing
light coming off it. Kids are on the banks making rafts
out of old junk, out of anything they can get their hands
on. Luděk wants to join them, to follow the other kids
and float like a white swan on the river. But Babi will kill
him. The river is so dirty, so full of rubbish. How do the
swans even survive? How do they live?

There is a huge hole in the pavement right on the corner,
and it goes down to some medieval underworld. Someone
put wooden guards around it, but that just makes kids
dare each other to climb over and get closer to the hole.
It happened when a big truck came thundering down the
street. Someone could have been sucked down if they were
standing on that spot. Someone could have been killed.

Babi told him to stay away. She said that the city was
falling to pieces. She put her hand on her forehead when
she said this. She could be dramatic as hell sometimes. But
Luděk loved the mess, the decay. His city wasn't clean, it

wasn't pretty. And there were wires everywhere in the sky and they crisscrossed like a million black lines. Everything was covered in stinking soot, in pigeon shit, covered in old rusted scaffolding, but Luděk did not want to live in a pretty doll's house. He did not want to live in the country and be bored to death in the fields.

Prague was his city, the flat his whole world, and he loved it all.

Luděk washed his face in the bathroom of their new house, and Max came in to see what he was doing. Max was the best of dogs, one of those dogs who was up for anything. Alert and ready. Max was his dog.

Luděk looked in the mirror. He studied his lips, his nose. Maybe he would look like Děda when he grew up. Or maybe he would look like his papa. Babi looked like Aunty Máňa, and Mama looked like Děda. Uncle Bohdan had Babi's face, her cheekbones. Luděk's baby sister didn't look like anyone yet – she was just a baby. Maybe she would look like Aleš.

Luděk closed his blue eyes, he shut them tight. He wanted to look like no one else at all. He wanted to be something completely new.

Max barked. He wanted to run.

'Okay,' Luděk said. 'Let's go!'

Melbourne
1981

The blue Ford Telstar pulled out of the garage and my grandpa switched on the radio. Talking – news – the haze of AM radio. Then a song came on that I knew, a flute and soft cymbals and a strumming guitar – 'Nights in White Satin'. I looked out of the window at all the cars and the trams and the life that rushed by. The song was like a long dream, like soft clouds moving inside your eyes. It was like floating – drifting. I could tell that my grandma was smiling even though I couldn't see her face properly from the back seat.

We were going to the airport.

We stood in the international arrivals hall and the automatic doors opened and closed – opened and closed. People came through in twos and threes. They looked dazed, pushing trolleys loaded up with suitcases. My grandma held my hand tight and her skin was sweaty. We waited.

My grandpa refused to get a trolley because they cost fifty cents. He said they should be free, that they were a public service, and how were you meant to find fifty cents if you'd just arrived from somewhere overseas.

'It's a rort,' he said. He would carry Aunty Eva's luggage, but he hoped to God she didn't bring too many suitcases.

She only had one, and when she came through the automatic magic doors, my grandma let go of my hand and started to cry. Aunty Eva cried, too. My grandpa and I just stood there waiting for the hugging and crying to end. It took a long time.

Aunty Eva.

I could not stop staring at her. She had the same face as my grandma's face. Their mouths the same, their lips downturned like an upside-down smile. Their eyes the same – large and brown with flecks of green deep inside. They both wore the same gold and garnet earrings that sparkled on their large earlobes. The ones that were like bright flowers made out of delicate petals of glistening red stone. The ones my grandma told me she had worn since she was very small.

One had to be repaired once because it fell on the floor in the bathroom and a tiny stone came loose. The man at the jewellery shop fixed it quickly, and he told my grandma there was no charge. He said the gold was very old, and that if my grandma ever wanted to sell the pair, he would be very interested. He noticed my grandma's ring – the one she let me try on sometimes. It was way too big, even for my thumb, and the gold band was always warm from my grandma's skin.

'Ruby?' the man asked and my grandma nodded, the fingers of her other hand rubbed the stone protectively.

'I cannot sell,' she said. 'Thank you.'

When we left the shop, my grandma put her earrings in right there on the street, finding the holes in her earlobes by feel. She looked like herself again. She stood taller.

'Malá Liška,' Aunty Eva said, and she picked me up and hugged me so tightly I couldn't breathe. When she put me down she took my hand, and it was so familiar. The feel of her skin, the size of her palm, the ruby ring on her wedding finger.

Aunty Eva sat in the front seat, and my grandma sat next to me. The sun was bright and Aunty Eva shielded her eyes with her hand. My grandpa flipped her sun visor down.

'It's a thirty-minute drive,' he said – in English. Aunty Eva lit a cigarette. It was already hot in the car and I wanted to put the window down, but my grandma never let me put the window down because the wind messed up her tightly hair-sprayed beehive. Grandpa let me put the window down if it was just us, but today I knew not to ask.

My grandma pointed out things on the way home – in Czech – and Aunty Eva nodded and nodded. We passed the huge cemetery with iron gates and old stones and angels that went on forever.

'People are dying to get in there,' my grandpa said – in English – and he winked at me in the rear-view mirror. It was what he always said when we passed that cemetery. Aunty Eva turned in her seat – *What?* she gestured with her arms, with her hands, and my grandma leaned forward and whacked my grandpa on the shoulder. 'Idiot!' she said – in English.

Aunty Eva lit another cigarette. She had a whole golden carton of them on her lap that she had bought duty free. I knew my grandpa would light a pipe as soon as we got home, and that he would be thinking about that right now. He said it was too hard to smoke a pipe and drive safely, but I knew it was because he knew the smoke made me feel a bit sick when we were in the car.

My grandpa made coffee in the kitchen, and my grandma studied the photos Aunty Eva handed her, one by one. She said something – in Czech – and Aunty Eva nodded, and then my grandma looked at me and said, 'He's getting big' – in English. She handed me the photo. A boy standing in the snow, wearing a parka just like mine, his eyes alive. And even though the photo was still, it was as if the boy was moving, buzzing, like he was about to run out of the photograph and into the room, panting and breathless.

'Luděk,' my grandma said. Aunty Eva nodded. She winked at me.

There were other photographs. A bright green car that looked like a spaceship from a cartoon. A man with a big belly standing next to a TV. A photo of Alena, her hair cut short – her hair not long and shiny anymore. A photo of a bridge, a castle, a river – just like the tapestry on the wall.

My grandpa came into the lounge room with a tray and put it down on the table. Coffee in the good cups, the cream and brown ones that had orange saucers. There was a small glass of milk for me and I drank it down. Aunty Eva pulled something out of her handbag, something wrapped loosely in tissues.

'For you,' she said – in English, her accent strong and sharp, and she unwrapped the tissues. Underneath, a little clay bird with holes down its sides. A little clay bird painted blue. Aunty Eva brought the tail of the bird to her lips and blew – her fingers moving over the holes. She played a tune, a song, and the happy notes flew out of the bird's open beak. I watched her face, and it was soft, her eyes closed.

She opened her eyes when the song was over. She held out the bluebird to me.

'Ocarina,' she said. 'I teach.' My grandma nodded and she said 'Later' – in English. Then she said, 'Say *thank you*.'

I took the ocarina in my hands carefully, like it was a real bird that might fly away. I hoped I would be able to make it sing like Aunty Eva could.

'Thank you,' I said – in Czech. This made my grandma smile.

I could say a few things in Czech. I could ask a few simple questions, but I did not always understand the answers. Sometimes I got the order of the words muddled up, and this made the adults laugh. I wished that I could speak better for my grandma. But my grandpa told me that it did not matter, and maybe I could just understand if I listened very carefully.

'That is the best way to learn,' he said. 'Just listen to the music of people talking, and you will understand the song.'

I'd sit in the lounge and listen to my grandma and her sister talk on and on – faster than I had ever heard. It was like they were five years old again and had secrets and a language all of their own. Sometimes I'd close my eyes and imagine pictures, shadows, a time long ago. *Remember our sled? Going down Petřín hill? Remember how Babi would snore all night and she sounded like a monster? Do you remember Mama's voice? Poor Papa – he worked so hard.*

And they would call each other soft names – nicknames. Máňa, Madlenka, Maruška, Mařenka, Majka, Márinka. Eva, Evka, Evička, Evinka, Evelína, Lina.

So many names – like soft snow falling. The days went by like this. The flat full of new happy songs. Songs from the past. But one day the song changed.

———⟨———

I'm in my spaceship – the upside-down cream footstool. There is no music playing, only the sound of the electric fan blowing warm air around the room, and my grandma and Aunty Eva talking on the couch, their voices getting faster, getting louder.

'You don't know what it's like. You don't know. You got out!' Aunty Eva stands up.

My grandma is silent. She stays on the couch.

Aunty Eva lights a cigarette and throws the lighter down on the coffee table. She paces the room.

'Papa lost an eye.'

'I know.'

'They hit him so hard.'

'I know.'

'They made him work as an undertaker.'

'I know.'

'It killed him, the war. It killed him!'

Silence.

Another cigarette. Aunty Eva blows a cloud of smoke up to the ceiling.

'It was all right for you,' she says. 'I was stuck.'

My grandma stands up now. She has turned into a huge bear on the inside like she does sometimes. A huge bear woken up too soon.

'I knew no one – nothing. I cried myself to sleep every night! I worked until my hands were raw every day!' Now my grandma is pointing at Aunty Eva. Pointing right at her face.

'And it was your fault I wasn't there – it was your fault I couldn't help Papa.'

I watch Aunty Eva, her face, but she gives nothing away. Her face is stone. She squashes her cigarette out in the ashtray and walks out of the room. I hear the front door shut, footsteps going down the stairs.

I stay still in my spaceship. My grandma looks at nothing. One of her fists is clenched – the ruby ring squeezed tight between her fingers. The moment goes on and then we hear the front door. But it's not Aunty Eva. It's my grandpa.

We looked, my grandpa and me.

We walked to the market and went to every stall. We walked up and down the main road on both sides and peered in every shop window. We looked in the park, down all the side streets, at the football oval. We looked in all the places that Aunty Eva could walk to on her own, but she was nowhere.

My grandpa's forehead was sweaty and he stopped to wipe it with his hanky. He said he didn't know where else to look. We stood on the street corner and he told me to run back to the flat and see if Aunty Eva had come home. I did, but she was not there. My grandma looked like she had been crying.

My grandpa put his hanky back in his pocket.

'Let's go back to the shops,' he said.

We had not looked at the supermarket, at the Safeway, because it was quite far down the main road. We had only been there once with Aunty Eva because my grandma wanted to get ice cream for dessert. She got the one that was on special – coffee flavour. I had never had coffee flavour and I didn't think it would be very good, but we never had ice cream so I was happy anyway.

The glass doors opened, the supermarket buzzing and bright, and there she was, standing near the cashiers, staring at all the items being put into bag after bag after bag. Aunty Eva. My grandpa touched her shoulder, said something in Czech, very softly – very close. I did not catch the words. Aunty Eva's face was still and pale and did not move. Then she blinked.

'Home,' she said.

We went home, walking slowly, and Aunty Eva did not speak. She went to bed as soon as we got to the flat, not looking at my grandma or at anything at all.

'She's not herself,' my grandpa said to me. And I did not know what that meant, but I saw her eyes, how she looked like she was in pain.

'She has never left her country before. Maybe there's too much water under the bridge.'

The bridges of Prague, the river flowing strongly.

The old city that I had never seen, but knew so well – the streets, the apartment buildings, the sky.

A small boy running, running – always running.

A white swan.

A little brown suitcase in an attic.

A black theatre of fluorescent light.

Aunty Eva stayed in the flat. She did not want to go out, she just wanted to go home.

'Home,' she said, over and over.

Home – to one kind of bread, one brand of milk, one type of apple. Home – with one type of coffee, one type of tea. How can people cope with so much choice? How can they choose every day?

She never knew, never understood what it was like, even though people had told her – her daughter, her sister. But somewhere deep inside, she believed in her country. The workers. The state. The system. Even though she was unhappy, even though she was stuck – it was a world she understood. She just wanted her flat, her radio, her Russian TV. She just wanted to sit in her kitchen and not have to think about the past or the future. She wanted to go back to the Kingdom of Forgetting. To go back to sleep. It was all she had known for so very long. It was too loud here, too shiny, too bright.

All the things she had missed. The world had passed her by. And now she was old.

I brought the clay bird into the kitchen and my grandma was making tea. I asked her if she could play a song like

Aunty Eva. My grandma took the bird in her hand, held it in her palm. She shook her head.

'This was our mother's,' she said. 'She died when we were just babies, and Eva and I both wanted this bird. We tried to share but it was no good, there were too many fights. My papa told me that Eva needed it more than I did. He said that I was stronger than her, and couldn't I give her this one thing. So, I did it for my papa.'

My grandma handed me back the bird.

'Papa was right to give it to her. She was really good at playing it.'

In the lounge, Aunty Eva sat and stared at nothing. She was going home tomorrow. She had already packed and now she was just waiting to leave.

I walked over and put a cup of tea on the coffee table. '*Čaj*,' I said.

She looked at me but her eyes were unfocused.

'Luděk,' she said.

'It's me,' I said.

'It's you,' she said.

I sat down next to her.

'Everybody gone.' She patted my hand.

I held the bluebird up to her. 'Will you play?' I asked.

She shook her head, but I put the bird on her lap anyway. I knew that it should go home with her even though I wanted to keep it very much. It belonged to her and maybe it would sing for no one else.

Maybe it wanted to go home, too.

They spoke in Czech, softly. Voices crisscrossed the room – over and over until I could no longer tell who was talking. They had become one person. A person who had lived two different lives – separated by so much distance – but one all the same.

And it was as if they were saying sorry to each other.

'I forgive you.'

'I know.'

'It's okay.'

'It's okay.'

And sometimes there was laughter and sometimes soft crying.

'I would never have survived like you have.'

'I am not strong like you.'

They fell asleep on the couch, heads touching, holding hands like children.

The Twins

1921

Two girls are born – identical. Prague, 1921.

When they are six months old their mother will die and a streak of hair near the centre of their forehead will turn white. That streak will stay for their whole lives. No relative had it before them and no relative will have it after them. It is theirs, and theirs alone.

One sister will keep her hair long. She will wear it up in public, but at home, she will let it loose because it reminds her of her childhood. The other sister will cut her hair short in 1968, and she will keep it short for the rest of her days. Short with a slight curl from rollers, from having it set. But the streak will still be there – clear and bright, right in the centre of her forehead.

A bolt of lightning.

Both sisters will wear the gold and garnet earrings they were given at birth until the day they die in 1991 – 15,769 kilometres apart.

A Pack of Cards

Cribbage is my grandpa's favourite game. It is very complicated and you have to add up in your head all the while as you go – *15–2, 15–4, 15–6, plus 3 for a run.* Grandpa is proud of me now I know how to play. Round and round our pegs move on the cribbage board that my grandpa carved himself. 'Streets ahead,' my grandpa says when his peg has rounded a corner ahead of mine. *I'm streets ahead.*

But right now my grandpa is teaching me how to play patience. It's so I can play cards by myself when there is no one to play with, or when my grandpa is working or sleeping or just smoking his pipe and resting. He says that patience is very good for your mind.

'When you play patience, you just concentrate on the game and the cards in front of you – one move at a time. It's all about the cards that are underneath, like an iceberg. The game is about the cards you cannot see.'

He shows me how to set the game up, how to count out the seven piles of cards. He tells me to count out loud. My grandma tells me to count out loud in Czech.

Jeden, dva, tři, čtyři, pět, šest, sedm.

Jeden, dva, tři, čtyři, pět, šest.

Jeden, dva, tři, čtyři, pět.

Jeden, dva, tři, čtyři.

Jeden, dva, tři.

Jeden, dva.

Jeden.

My grandpa lived on for longer than my grandma. He missed her. He missed everything.

I didn't visit him often enough, in his tiny council flat – Prague still with him in the small living room. We played cards sometimes. He still enjoyed smoking his pipe.

The last time I saw him he was in hospital, and he looked small. He grabbed my hand.

'Malá Liška,' he said. 'It's you.'

'It's me,' I said. 'Little Fox.'

In the end, my grandpa just spoke Czech. He was no longer Bill – but Vilém once more.

A Smiths gold watch.

A wooden cribbage board.

A ruby ring.

A little brown suitcase.

A pack of playing cards.

All I have left of them.

When I hold the cards in my hand, when I bring them to my face, they smell exactly like that third storey flat, even after all these years – pipe tobacco, and the smell of butter and salt and something frying golden in the pan. I'm back in the place that was my whole world, with the two people I loved the most.

I play patience to be with them again, my grandma and grandpa.

I play patience and I'm sitting in the lounge room and everything is still. The coffee table, the TV with the lace doily on top, the sofa underneath the double windows, the gas heater, the mantlepiece, the framed tapestry of a city far away – with bridges and a river and a castle and a dark sky.

My grandpa is sleeping, his arm stretched out on the armrest of his chair. I lean my head down to his wrist. His watch is ticking, ticking, ticking so fast, the simple machines inside turning, turning.

Time running on. And I wish that I could slow it down. I wish that I could stop time.

The radio is on, classical music, and sometimes a sad song comes on – a violin weeping – and sometimes a triumphant marching tune blasts through to lift up the room.

My grandma calls out from the kitchen – lunch is ready, and my grandpa stands up, stretches his back. He takes my hand. We walk together to the kitchen for our lunch – a Kaiser roll with a slice of cheese and a slice of Pariser, a whole dill gherkin on the side. One gherkin for me, one for my grandma and one for my grandpa.

Author's note

This novel is a work of fiction, but my grandparents were very real. They taught me about kindness and gave me all the time and love I needed. They are never far from my thoughts.

My amazing cousin, Martin Schönweitz, spent hours answering my many questions about everything from soft drinks to communism in the 1980s. The Prague scenes would be nothing without his help. Martin, I am so grateful for all of your stories and time – I could not have written this book without you! I owe you 1000 beers.

Jiří Srnec is a very real person (born in 1931). He created the unique Black Light Theatre. I have called him The Magician in this novel for my own secret reasons.

Two small sections of this novel were published as short fiction – 'The Gherkin Jar' in the *Griffith Review*, Issue 61, and 'Melbourne 1980' in *Island* magazine, Issue 157. I would like to thank these journals for their ongoing support. How lucky we are to have such amazing journals in Australia.

The legend of the statue of Atlas is a traditional folk tale of Prague.

Acknowledgements

I would like that thank the following people from the bottom of my heart:

My brilliant friend and publisher Vanessa Radnidge – how lucky I am to have you! Thank you for always being there.

Louise Sherwin-Stark – your support means so much to me. Thank you for getting behind this book.

Rebecca Allen – thank you for putting up with my old-school editing style and colour code. You did an incredible job.

To the whole amazing team at Hachette Australia, you are the best! Fiona Hazard, Chris Sims, Daniel Pilkington, Sean Cotcher, Anna Egelstaff, Lillian Kovats, Katrina Collett, Robert Watkins, Brigid Mullane, Stacey Clair, Deonie Fiford, Isabel Staas, Jenny Topham, Ella Chapman, Emma Rusher, Tom Saras and everyone who helped with this book.

Julia Styles – once again you have proved invaluable. You are a star.

My husband, David – you have endured another book with patience and love. You truly are the best person I know.

Martin Schönweitz – I can't wait to see you.

Karena Reid for the information and photos.

Jindra Cabelka – last keeper of the history.

Robert Farkas for my fox.

Christa Moffitt for my cover.

Marjorie Dalvean for the Black Light Theatre catalogues and photographs.

My writing group – Janey, Helen, Lis and Cath.

Lastly, my brilliant friends and family: Linda Graham, Amanda Graham, James Parrett, Chiyoko Parrett, Charlie Kneale, Haruki Parrett, Ikumi Parrett, Lyn Armanasco, Steve Cue, Jacinda Pfeffer, Janine Foote, Mary Viane, Paul Karanja, August Shan, Charles Njoroge, Gerald Gichana, Sarah Winman, Maxine Beneba Clarke, Jikara Liddy, Ivana Pugliese, Adam Bourke, Megan O'Brien and Melisinka Winterson.